A Forgotten Shadow

A FORGOTTEN SHADOW

A CHIEF INSPECTOR SHADOW MYSTERY

H L Marsay

TULE
PUBLISHING

DEDICATION

For Harry,
With love x

CHAPTER ONE

Down 3. Yes Dr I count in the great outdoors (11 letters)

DETECTIVE CHIEF INSPECTOR John Shadow stared out across the heather-covered moor. He watched as the August sun blazed down on the tweed-clad gamekeeper strolling back towards his Land Rover. With his collection of excited spaniels and Labradors bounding alongside him, he turned and gave Shadow a friendly wave goodbye. It was a quintessential English summer scene, and Shadow would have appreciated it more, were it not for the dead body lying in the copse behind him.

He was still feeling queasy from having to look at it. The image was imprinted on his brain. The blackened gunshot wound to the victim's head, the thick, congealing blood, and the buzzing flies that began landing on the body as soon as the plastic sheet was raised. Shadow shuddered. He took another deep breath and fished out an indigestion tablet from the pocket of his battered old wax jacket that he always wore.

When he'd left *Florence*—his narrow boat—that morning, a low mist had been hovering over the river, giving no hint that it would turn out to be one of the hottest days of the year. So now, on top of everything else, he was sweltering. He popped the chalky tablet into his mouth and waited for it to dissolve. Hopefully, it would help settle his churning stomach. The large and delicious steak pie he'd consumed a couple of hours ago was now starting to feel like a mistake.

He had been enjoying a leisurely late lunch in the beer garden of The Lamb and Lion, sitting alone in the shade of the city walls. Just as he had been about to complete the last clue of the *Yorkshire Post* crossword, his deputy, Sergeant Jimmy Chang, had appeared with his usual impeccable timing and informed him that a body had been discovered on the Duke of Kirkdale's estate. Recent cuts to the policing budget meant that neither Thirsk nor Easingwold, the stations closest to the estate, had an officer senior enough to attend, so the call had come through to York.

Therefore, a little over an hour's drive through the North Yorkshire countryside later, Shadow and Jimmy arrived on the moors above Kirkdale village, where Greenwood, the duke's gamekeeper, was waiting for them. Shadow had made the introductions then Greenwood had led the two detectives to a small copse on the edge of the moor where the body of a man who looked to be between forty or fifty years old was lying next to a shotgun. A few uniformed officers from Easingwold were already on the scene and had begun cordoning the area off. Greenwood informed Jimmy and Shadow that the deceased's name was Flynn FitzAllan.

"He and his wife train racehorses including His Grace's, or at least he did. Mr FitzAllan's stables are down at the Grange. He rents the place off the estate," the gamekeeper continued to explain.

"What was he doing up here on the moor?" asked Shadow. Greenwood looked down at the gun and then back to the two policemen.

"Well, it's the Glorious Twelfth today isn't it?" he replied as if the answer was obvious.

"What's that?" asked Jimmy, looking up from the notes he had been taking. The gamekeeper stared at him with his mouth open. Shadow stepped in.

"Today is the twelfth of August and so it is the beginning of the grouse shooting season. It's known as the Glorious Twelfth, Sergeant," he explained patiently.

"Exactly," said Greenwood. "His Grace was hosting a small shooting party to mark the occasion. There's a party at the castle tonight and a much larger shoot due to take place next week. This business won't interfere with that will it?"

"I hope not, Mr Greenwood," replied Shadow briskly. "So Mr FitzAllan was up here shooting grouse with how many other people?"

"Oh, let me think now." The gamekeeper began silently counting on his fingers. "Including Mr FitzAllan there were five guns and four loaders and about half a dozen beaters. We stopped for lunch, then at about half past one, Mr FitzAllan left the others to either make or take a phone call,

I'm not sure which. The rest of us started the afternoon's drive, but when he hadn't returned after about half an hour, I sent a loader to look for him, my son in fact. That's when we found the body, Chief Inspector. It's a real shame. He was having a good day too; he easily bagged the most birds."

"Didn't anyone hear or see anything?" asked Shadow.

The gamekeeper shook his head. "No, Chief Inspector. You can't see the copse from up on the moor and I guess he must have been hit after the shooting started again; plus we were all wearing ear defenders."

Shadow glanced down at the dead man's open hands then his eyes travelled over the long grass surrounding the body. Lying a few inches away was a mobile phone with its screen badly smashed.

"What happened to his phone? Did someone stand on it?" he asked. The gamekeeper looked a little perplexed.

"Why no, I don't think so. We were all very careful. Like I said Giles was the first to find him, then I arrived and the others. I thought it best not to touch him. I mean, it was obvious he was dead."

"Quite right, Mr Greenwood," replied Shadow. "Can you tell us the names of everyone else who was up here?"

"His Grace and Mr FitzAllan, then Lord and Lady East-wold, that's His Grace's sister-in-law and her husband in case you didn't know, and Sir Charles Richmond."

Shadow recognised the last name. Sir Charles was the local member of parliament. He flicked his eyes across to check Jimmy was noting everything down as the gamekeeper continued to talk.

"I was here of course and Giles, my son, it was him who phoned you by the way. The other loaders were all local lads: Wilf Sugden, Rory Stanwick and Fred Houlston. They're all good lads, same with the beaters, Chief Inspector. They were over on the other side of the moor all day. I kept in contact with them over the radio and told them to go home when we found Mr FitzAllan, but I've got a list here with their names and numbers." He handed a creased sheet of paper to Shadow. "I can vouch for them all," the gamekeeper insisted.

"I'm sure you can, but we may still need them to make a statement," said Shadow passing the list on to Jimmy after giving it a brief glance.

"Sorry, what are beaters and loaders?" asked Jimmy.

The gamekeeper looked as him with a degree of sympathy. "Well, Sergeant, loaders load the guns, so as to save time for those who are shooting," he explained slowly, "and beaters flush out the birds into the path of the guns, usually with the help of dogs." He gestured to the pack of spaniels and Labradors who were waiting patiently where he'd left them on the edge of the crime scene.

"Have you worked for the duke long, Mr Greenwood?" asked Shadow before Jimmy had chance to make another enquiry. It was obvious that as far as the gamekeeper was concerned his sergeant may as well be wearing a T-shirt with the words 'I am a townie' printed across it.

"All my life. At least since I left school that is. I grew up here in Kirkdale. My father was gamekeeper to His Grace before me. He trained me up. All the years we've been organising shoots, we've never had anything like this happen before though, Chief Inspector. Poor Mr FitzAllan." The gamekeeper briefly removed his flat cap and wiped the back of his hand across his brow. He was clearly bothered by the day's events and the chief inspector thought it was time to let him get back to his dogs.

"Thank you very much for your help, Mr Greenwood," said Shadow, holding out his hand again. "We'll be in touch if we have any further questions."

WHEN THE GAMEKEEPER had left them the two detectives approached the dead man for a closer look. It was impossible to say if Flynn FitzAllan had been murdered, committed suicide or had been the victim of a terrible shooting accident. Although Shadow had been in the police for over thirty years, encountering a death by shooting in North Yorkshire was still rare. He would need to wait and hear from the pathologist and the forensics team to determine if a crime had been committed. He gestured to a uniformed officer, who placed the cover back over the body. Shadow took a few steps back. The phone was a puzzle. Had the victim heard bad news and smashed it in frustration before taking his own life? Or did the killer try and destroy it? But if that were the case why not take it with them?

"What do you think, Chief?" asked Jimmy eagerly, interrupting his thoughts. As usual his sergeant was dressed in jeans and a black leather jacket despite the heat, but today he was also sporting a pair of designer sunglasses that Shadow suspected were as expensive as his trainers. "We don't get many GSWs," Jimmy continued. "This is pretty exciting."

"Many what?" asked Shadow irritably.

"GSWs, Chief. Gunshot wounds."

Shadow sighed. His deputy had obviously been watching one of the American crime dramas he was so fond of.

"You do know it's actually quicker just to say shot, don't you?"

"Is it, Chief?" Jimmy began mouthing *GSW* and *shot* to himself. "Maybe it's abbreviated to differentiate between getting shot by a gun instead of something else, like an arrow say."

"Yes, I'm sure it will be very useful if Robin Hood and his Merry Men ever make a comeback," muttered Shadow, the flies and blood making him feel too nauseous to press the point. He walked further away from the deceased and spent a few quiet moments staring out across the moors, leaving Jimmy to liaise with the uniformed officers who were continuing to tape off the area.

He watched as the gamekeeper drove away. In the distance he could see the White Horse of Kilburn carved into the chalk escarpment of Sutton Bank and further to his right lay the ruins of Byland Abbey. Closer, only about twenty yards away, between the road and the edge of the moor was another ruin. An old chapel covered in ivy and with half its roof missing. These landmarks were all familiar to him, but he was struggling to recall the exact time he'd last seen them; it must have been soon after his mother died. His thoughts were interrupted again by his sergeant.

"Chief! Dr Donaldson is here."

Shadow turned to see Jimmy motioning towards the track the gamekeeper had just driven down. A little way behind his sergeant, Shadow could see the unmistakable figure of Dr Donaldson stepping out of his Volvo. The pathologist began pulling on a protective suit over his immaculate shirt and waistcoat. With a reluctant sigh, Shadow trudged back towards the corpse in the copse.

"This is more like it, Shadow," declared the doctor loudly. He rubbed his hands together as he strode towards the body. Shadow noted that he had also protected his gleaming patent leather shoes with plastic covers. "I don't mind being dragged out into the sticks for something a little more interesting than the usual drunks drowning in the Ouse or the junkies overdosing that you bring me." He glanced around hopefully. "Is His Grace not here? I understood the deceased was a guest of his."

"Sadly not. You'll have to hone your social skills another time. Now if you don't mind, could you get on and tell me exactly what we are investigating? I need you to confirm the time of death too. We've been told somewhere between one thirty and two."

"If anyone needs to hone their social skills around here, it's you, Shadow," retorted Donaldson. "Step back and give me some space so I can work. I don't require an audience, thank you."

Shadow took several paces back, privately grateful not to have to stand too close to the body while the pathologist knelt down and began to poke and prod. Instead he returned to admiring the view. Jimmy appeared by his side, his phone held aloft in front of him.

"What are you doing?" asked Shadow.

"Taking a few photos to show Sophie how nice it is out here. I'm going to try and convince her that we should move to the countryside after we get married."

Shadow raised an eyebrow. Sophie was the other pathologist they worked with and also Jimmy's fiancée.

"She grew up on a farm, didn't she? I'm sure she's aware of what the countryside looks like, Sergeant."

"Maybe, but I still think she'll like to see where we've been. It's a shame I can't take a photo of the body too. She doesn't get the chance to see many GSWs either. She'll be gutted Donaldson got the call for this one. Hey, I bet he hasn't seen many either, maybe he'll ask Soph, for a second opinion," continued Jimmy hopefully.

"If he does, you'll need to keep your camera turned on."

"Why's that, Chief?"

"To take a photo of all the pigs flying by."

"You can rule out suicide, Shadow," proclaimed Donaldson loudly behind them. Shadow turned to see the doctor had now stood up again and was peeling off his latex gloves. "He was shot twice. Once in the back and then the wound to the head. I concur with the time of death you proposed."

Reluctantly Shadow returned to study the body. Looking at the front of the man there was no sign of injury to his body, but now the doctor had half turned him on his side, a dark patch of blood was clearly visible on the back of his shirt. Donaldson cleared his throat and continued with his pronouncements. Despite stating he didn't want an audience, Shadow knew the doctor enjoyed nothing more than making theatrical declarations about his findings.

"The entry wounds are noticeably different. The wound to the back is actually several small punctate injuries where the pellets have been dispersed, but no burn marks or tattooing of the skin, leading me to conclude that the first shot must have been fired from over ten metres away. The angle of entry is odd. I would hazard a guess that the victim was walking up and down as he spoke on his phone—" the doctor gestured to the smashed mobile "—and therefore the killer had to hit a moving target, before finishing him off with the second shot. The second entry wound to the head is a single smooth margined circle." Donaldson knelt down using his fountain pen pointed towards the head wound to emphasise his words. "There are also signs of singeing and tattooing, with possible traces of plastic and metal from the cartridge in the tract, therefore this second shot was fired from less than thirty centimetres away, probably when he'd already fallen to the ground judging by the angle of entry. There are no exit wounds for either injury."

"So, the bullets are still in the victim?" asked Jimmy as he entered all the details in his electronic notebook. Donaldson scowled at him. He hated to be interrupted mid flow.

"There are no bullets, Sergeant. Weren't you listening?" the doctor replied impatiently his lips curling into a slight sneer. "We aren't dealing with some sort of inner-city gangland killing. The weapon used is a smooth-barrelled shotgun. They do not fire a single projectile, but cartridges full of multiple pellets. Depending on the cartridges used, the pellets are between two millimetres and nine millimetres. I don't claim to be a ballistics expert, but I would expect the pellets used here to be at the lower end of the scale. I take it you don't know what cartridges are compatible with this gun? I assume it belonged to the deceased."

He pointed to the gun next to the body and Shadow nodded to confirm this.

Donaldson glanced around and raised an eyebrow. "And no sign of any spent cartridges either?"

This time Shadow shook his head trying to ignore the superior look on Donaldson's face.

"I see." The doctor sighed. "As usual you've been very

little help, but you are fortunate that I will be able to provide you with the details you require after the post-mortem; however, I can confidently say, in my opinion, you are definitely dealing with a case of murder. My guess is that the pellets that entered through his back are lodged in his ribs. It's possible some got through to his heart and the second lot will need to be fished out of his brains."

Shadow winced. He was struggling to hold back the bile rising in his throat. Jimmy was staring at the gun on the floor, a look of confusion on his face.

"If you think the bullets—sorry, Doctor, the pellets— might have come from the victim's gun, then even if it's not suicide, maybe it could still be an accident. Could he have dropped his gun and it went off by mistake? Maybe ricocheted or something?" Jimmy suggested, only to be met by a snort of derision from Donaldson.

Shadow frowned. It was one thing for him to be exasperated by Jimmy's stream of unlikely theories, but quite another for anyone else to pass judgement on them.

"I doubt it, Sergeant," he replied, trying with great effort to keep his tone neutral. He did wish Jimmy would sometimes engage his brain before his mouth. "Not now the good doctor has found two gunshot wounds. Nobody shoots themselves accidentally twice."

"Quite," snapped Donaldson. "Well, I refuse to work in this heat any longer. I'll let you know what else I discover when I've had a look at him on the slab. Good day, gentlemen."

With that he strode back towards his car. The two detectives watched him gesture impatiently to one of the constables, who hurriedly lifted the yellow and black tape out of his way.

"Maybe one of the shooting party wasn't much of a shot and instead of hitting a bird, their pellets or cartridges or whatever hit Mr FitzAllan instead. They might not have even realised," suggested Jimmy again.

"Perhaps," sighed Shadow. "We would of course know a lot more if our forensics team had bothered to show up. Where the hell are those two?" he asked irritably. The forensics team was led by two young, slightly chaotic scientists called Ben and Ollie, but Shadow privately referred to them as Laurel and Hardy. They may be highly qualified scientists, but they seemed to struggle with the more basic day-to-day tasks.

"Oh, I got a text from Ben. They're a bit lost. Their sat nav sent them the wrong way, but they should be here soon."

"For crying out loud," grumbled Shadow. "Aren't either of them capable of reading a map?" Jimmy opened his mouth to reply, but Shadow held up his hand to stop him. "I'm not wasting any more time waiting for them. Tell them what Donaldson said and get them to focus on FitzAllan's gun. I want to know what sort of cartridges it takes and if they can tell me how recently it was fired. I also want to know if they can work out where whoever fired the gun was standing."

They began walking back to their car in silence until Jimmy had finished sending the text message to Ben.

"Donaldson seemed pretty disappointed the duke wasn't here," said Jimmy when he'd put his phone away.

"That's because Donaldson is a snob, who is impressed by titles." Shadow snorted.

"Don't you think it was a bit weird that the duke left his gamekeeper to tell us one of his guests was dead?" continued Jimmy.

"I think you'll find that the aristocracy are a law unto themselves. They are used to having servants take care of things for them, especially if those things happen to be particularly unpleasant or inconvenient tasks. However, as it now appears his guest's wounds weren't self-inflicted, I think we should have a word with His Grace, after we've spoken to Mr FitzAllan's widow."

For now, Shadow wasn't prepared to discuss with his sergeant what was really occupying his thoughts. It wasn't the duke's behaviour he found strange, but that of his gamekeeper, Greenwood. He took his place in the passenger seat while Jimmy drove them back down the narrow winding lane towards the village of Kirkdale.

"It's nice being out here in the countryside isn't it, Chief? All the space and fresh air and wildlife. I hardly ever left the city before I met Sophie, but you look like you belong here. You blend right in. You've even got the same jacket as the gamekeeper. Don't you think it feels like being on holiday?"

"Does encountering a dead body often occur when you go on holiday, Sergeant?" asked Shadow as he stared out the window.

"Um no, apart from that I mean, but it could still turn out to be an accident."

Shadow only grunted in response. His sergeant's unfailing enthusiasm combined with the heat was exhausting him. For the chief inspector, the visit to this part of North Yorkshire felt less like a holiday and more of a trip down memory lane. His grandparents had lived at Church Farm in Kirkdale, and his father had been the village policeman. However, he only had vague recollections of the place. He and his mother had moved away after his father had been killed when Shadow was very young. He had been shot in the woods on the duke's estate when he had gone to investigate reports of poaching. That's why he found Greenwood the gamekeeper's behaviour so strange. Shadow was a relatively unusual name. Greenwood had told them he'd always lived in the village and must have heard about his father's death, yet he hadn't commented when Shadow had introduced himself. He'd even gone on to say that nothing like FitzAllan's death had ever occurred before, yet one of the few facts Shadow knew about what happened to his father was that Greenwood was the name of the person who had reported the crime. Shadow now assumed it was the current gamekeeper's father.

They drove over a narrow stone bridge then slowed while they passed a line of skittish, sweaty racehorses making their way back from the gallops. The lead rider lifted her crop in thanks. Then they continued along the winding country road edged by drystone walls and passed the old millstone bearing the name of the village. Shadow continued to stare silently out of the window. It had been years since he had visited Kirkdale, but he recognised the pub—the DeVere Arms—and the small cottage where he and his parents had lived for the first few years of his life. They carried on past St Michael's Church, where Shadow's parents had been married, and he had been christened. As they drove on Jimmy continued to wax lyrical about the countryside, the stone cottages with their pretty gardens and the unusual octagonal tower of the church, while Shadow tried to ignore him.

Next to the church was the farm where his grandparents had lived, but to Shadow it was barely recognisable. The barn where the cows had slept in the winter and the sheds where he'd helped to bottle feed orphaned lambs had been turned into "luxury holiday lets" as the sign on the gate told him. Shadow sighed quietly to himself. These days it seemed tourism was more profitable than farming.

The Grange was located on the edge of the village. It was a large square Georgian house, built of York stone. The long driveway was dotted with signs that read "slow" and "caution horses", and in the padlocks on either side, bays, chestnuts and greys stood in the sun enjoying the lush grass. Shadow and Jimmy pulled up in front of the white panelled front door and got out.

Shadow lifted the wrought-iron knocker, rapped on the door and waited. There was no answer. Jimmy pointed to a black-and-white signpost on the edge of the drive. It read "stable yard" and pointed down a path leading to the back of the house. Shadow nodded and the two detectives trudged along the path that led to the rear of the house where they found a yard surrounded on each side by stables, their occupant's long faces peering out of their stalls, their ears twitching at the sound of the new arrivals. In the middle of the yard a group of young men and women, mostly dressed in jodhpurs and T-shirts were huddled around a stack of straw bales. Two of the girls were sobbing loudly.

One of the group noticed Shadow and Jimmy's arrival and gestured towards them. A young woman came hurrying over. Unlike the others she was wearing a short denim skirt and vest top with her wellies. Her sunglasses were on the top of her head, holding back her long dark hair and her eyes were red from crying.

"Can I help you gentlemen?" she asked in a soft Irish accent.

"I'm Chief Inspector Shadow and this is Sergeant Chang. We were hoping to speak with Mrs FitzAllan," Shadow began to explain. The young woman's lip began to tremble, but she took a deep breath to compose herself.

"You're here about Flynn, aren't you? As you can see, we

are all very upset," she said pointing to the group behind her.

Shadow nodded. "Then I take it you've already heard about what happened, er Mrs FitzAllan?" Shadow ventured. He thought she looked too young to be married to the dead man, but he'd been wrong in these matters before. The young woman, however, shook her head and held out her hand.

"No, I'm Clancy Kelly, Flynn's... I mean Mr FitzAllan's secretary. My boyfriend was one of the loaders at the shoot. He phoned to tell me what happened."

"Would that be Giles, Wilf, Rory or Fred?" asked Jimmy scrolling back through his notes.

"Giles. Giles Greenwood. He was pretty shaken up. I couldn't believe it when he told me. None of us can believe it. I was only talking to Flynn this morning, just before he left for the castle."

"How did he seem? Did you think he was worried or anxious about anything?" asked Shadow.

"No, he was on good form like always. Laughing and joking with a couple of the lads."

"Did anyone telephone him from here?"

"No, he always had his mobile with him, but I'm the only one who would have called him, and I wouldn't bother him when he's shooting unless there was a real emergency."

Clancy looked like she was on the brink of tears again, so Shadow hurried on. "And where is Mrs FitzAllan? Has she been informed of her husband's death?"

"Siobhan is in York. As I'm sure you know, Chief Inspector, the Ebor Festival starts tomorrow, so she and Aidan, our head stable lad, drove over with a one of our horses who is down to run. He's a little highly strung and not too keen on travelling, so Siobhan always tries to make sure he has time to settle down before a big race," Clancy explained, then paused as if she was choosing her next words carefully. "Naturally, I phoned Siobhan as soon as we heard the news, but I don't think she's planning on returning until later this evening, assuming the horse settles that is."

"I see," replied Shadow, wondering what sort of woman Siobhan FitzAllan was if she put the welfare of a horse before the death of her husband. "Well perhaps we could speak with her tomorrow?"

"The morning would probably be best, Chief Inspector, before Siobhan leaves for York again," said Clancy, looking a little apologetic. Shadow thanked her for her time and the two detectives turned to go.

Jimmy waited until they were out of earshot before he spoke. "It's a bit weird his wife hasn't rushed home isn't it, Chief?" he whispered.

Shadow shrugged. "I'd say unusual rather than weird, but perhaps she's very dedicated to her work," he suggested and nodded towards the glossy horses gazing in the paddocks. "These horses are worth a fortune and the Ebor is one of the biggest festivals in the racing calendar. She must have a lot of responsibility to the owners; perhaps she's just trying to be professional."

Jimmy shook his head. "Sophie's really professional, but I don't think she'd continue with a post-mortem if she'd just heard I'd been shot."

"Then perhaps the behaviour of Siobhan tells us everything we need to know about the state of the FitzAllans' marriage."

THE TWO DETECTIVES drove away from the stables and were heading back through the village, when Jimmy's phone began to bleep.

"Anything?" asked Shadow, as his sergeant pulled on to the verge to check his messages.

"Ben and Ollie are at the scene now, Chief. Do you want to go and see them?"

"Not remotely, but I suppose we must." Shadow sighed. "There's always the possibility they might surprise me and actually discover something useful."

They arrived back at the copse and waited silently for a moment alongside the uniformed officers who had removed their caps and bowed their heads as the body was finally removed by a private ambulance. Ben, the tall and thin forensic scientist, was standing with his hands on his hips staring into the distance, while Ollie, his short, tubby colleague, was hunched over peering intently at the ground.

"What can you tell me?" asked Shadow abruptly.

The two scientists turned around as if they were surprised to see the chief investigating officer.

"Oh, hello there, Chief. Hi, Jimmy," said Ben. "Bit of a puzzle actually. Jimmy told us what Donaldson thought about the size of shot that killed him, but we need to be sure. We really need to see the pellets that killed him, but Donaldson is going to need to remove them from the victim first. I think they'll be in his liver, but Ollie reckons the lungs."

Shadow fought against the wave of nausea and impatience that swept over him as Ollie began to speak.

"You see there are no cartridge shells here in the copse. We did find a fragment of a cartridge cap—" he held up an evidence bag containing a small piece of gold-coloured metal "—but we don't know how long it's been here for. Obviously, there are plenty of shells up by the butts, but…"

"If you'll pardon the pun," interrupted Ben with a laugh, before quickly stopping when he saw Shadow's scowl and Ollie continued.

"But we've checked them and apart from the ones used in the victim's gun, the other cartridges are all too big or rather the pellets inside them are; that's assuming Donaldson is right."

"So, it looks as though the killer took the spent cartridges with them," said Shadow wearily. As usual with his young forensics team, he was getting nowhere fast, not that either of them seemed perturbed by the lack of progress.

"The really interesting thing, though, is the victim's gun. It's an antique Lumley. Extremely rare," said Ben enthusiastically.

"What do you know about guns?" asked Shadow sceptically.

"My grandfather used to collect them," replied Ben, picking up FitzAllan's gun and looking at it with something close to affection before carefully placing it into an evidence bag. "Whenever I went to visit him, he'd spend hours showing them to me and telling me all about them."

"And what's so interesting about FitzAllan's gun?" said Shadow.

"Well, you see for a start, all the other guns were twelve bores, but his is a twenty bore. The Lumley is a smaller gun, hence the different cartridges. They were one of the first companies to make a gun light enough for a woman to shoot with at the beginning of the twentieth century. They were really popular after the First World War. Lots of soldiers who had lost a hand or an arm could still use them. I bet this model is nearly a hundred years old."

Shadow raised an eyebrow. The scientist sounded like he could be right for once.

"Did you check to see if the victim's gun was loaded?" he asked. Ben nodded his head.

"We did and it isn't. He had a few unused cartridges in his pocket, but no sign of any others. We wondered if his loader or the gamekeeper had taken them away."

"All right, we'll check," said Shadow. "Do you know which direction the shots that killed him came from?"

"From the east, so towards where the other guns were standing, but they would have been facing the other way. There's no chance one of them could have turned around and fired in this direction without the others noticing," said Ben sounding unusually emphatic.

"Maybe they were all in on it?" suggested Jimmy, briefly looking up from taking notes. Shadow shook his head impatiently and Ben seemed to share his scepticism.

"No, even if one of them had fired over here, I think the range is too far. We'll measure it, Chief, but whoever shot him would need to be about twenty metres away at the most. At a guess I would say the other guns were over a hundred metres away."

"Good. Phone Jimmy if you find anything else," replied Shadow, for once impressed by his forensic team. Who would have thought one of them would turn out to be something of a gun expert? He turned to leave. "That reminds me, do you think you'll be able to salvage anything from his phone?"

"We'll try our best, Chief. It's pretty badly smashed up, but we still managed to turn it on," replied Ollie. "We found another phone in his pocket too."

"Are they both his?"

"We need to run some tests, but we think so. The smashed-up one is registered to him and looks like the one he used all the time, but the other one looks like it's a burner."

"That means it's a prepaid mobile, without a contract, so it's difficult to trace the owner," added Ben.

"Yes, thank you, Ben, I do know what a burner is," snapped Shadow. Honestly, even when they were being helpful, they still hadn't lost their ability to irritate him. "Apparently he was on the phone before he was killed. Find out who he was in contact with. We're going back to the village to interview some more witnesses."

Chapter Two

Down 2. Don't scare the horses or they won't win here (5 letters)

WHEN SHADOW AND Jimmy left the murder scene for the second time, they drove back towards Kirkdale but before they reached the village, they turned left through a pair of large wrought-iron gates. The gates were flanked on either side by a small gatehouse and marked the entrance to the long, gravelled drive that led to Kirkdale Castle, the vast stone edifice that loomed ahead of them. It had originally been a Norman fort, built almost a thousand years ago, but over the years it had been rebuilt and extended by the DeVere family, who had risen from being mere barons to become the Dukes of Kirkdale.

The DeVeres had crossed the Channel with William the Conqueror back in 1066. To thank them for their support in the Norman invasion, the king had granted them vast swathes of land in North Yorkshire as well as the titles they still held. The subsequent generations had increased their wealth and social standing through prudent marriages and a knack of choosing the winning side whenever the fate of the crown was in doubt. The current Duke of Kirkdale, Albert

Alexander Louis St John DeVere, but known to his friends as Bertie had inherited the title five years ago upon the death of his father, Alexander, the twelfth duke.

The two detectives arrived at the front of the castle and stepped out of the car. Jimmy gave a long low whistle.

"Wow this place is huge. Do you think we should use the servants' entrance, Chief?"

"No," replied Shadow as he began to trudge up the flight of stone steps that led up to the four-columned portico. "We're not servants and besides, we'd probably get lost trying to find it."

"I think I should have worn a smarter jacket," said Jimmy jogging after him and self-consciously lowering his zip a little to show the shirt and tie he was wearing underneath.

"I've been telling you that for years," muttered Shadow.

A BUTLER WITH sleek grey hair and a supercilious expression answered the door and showed them into a magnificent hallway. Their footsteps echoed loudly as they crossed the marble floor. The room was full of antique furniture and two full suits of armour stood on either side of a huge fireplace. All around the walls, portraits of dukes and duchesses from the past gazed down at them. Liveried servants hurried back and forth carrying trays of glasses and crockery.

"Please wait here, gentlemen. I shall inform His Grace

that you wish to speak with him," said the butler.

Shadow nodded politely. "Thank you, Mr?"

"Jarvis, sir, just Jarvis."

"I've never met a real-life butler before, Chief, or a duke. Do you think we should bow?" asked Jimmy under his breath. Before Shadow could answer, he heard a voice above their heads.

"It's all right, Jarvis. I'll deal with this," said a voice in a cool clear tone that sounded as though it was used to being obeyed. The butler inclined his head slightly and then disappeared through a door fitted into one of the wooden panels of the wall without another word. Shadow looked up. Standing at the top of the sweeping cantilever staircase was the tall, elegant figure of Annabel DeVere, Duchess of Kirkdale. She stared down at Shadow and Jimmy as if they were two Labradors that had rolled in something particularly unpleasant. Shadow recognised her immediately from her photographs that regularly appeared in the *Yorkshire Post*. He recalled she had once been the Honourable Annabel Wantage—a socialite and successful fashion model—before her marriage to the duke a little over a year ago.

"Good afternoon," he said politely. "I am Chief Inspector Shadow, and this is Sergeant Chang. We are investigating the death of Mr FitzAllan."

The duchess didn't reply; instead she seemed to silently glide down the stairs. She was wearing a long black satin gown that made her pale skin look almost white. Her blonde hair was piled on top of her head in a way that was meant to look effortless, but Shadow suspected it was anything but. Diamonds sparkled at her throat and on her ears and fingers. When she stopped in front of them, she was almost as tall as Jimmy.

"Couldn't this have waited? We are expecting guests this evening," she said as she gestured to a young man laden down with plates.

"I apologise, Your Grace, but as I said we are investigating the unexplained death of one of your guests. May we ask you a few questions about Mr FitzAllan? Did you know him well?"

"He wasn't my guest. I loathe shooting. You'll need to make an appointment if you wish to speak with my husband."

Shadow noted she hadn't answered his question.

"Perhaps we could wait here until your guests arrive. If His Grace is too busy to see us this evening, it's possible some of them could assist us instead."

Annabel narrowed her eyes at Shadow and drew her mouth into a thin line.

"Come with me. He's in the library."

As they followed Annabel down a long corridor lined with oil paintings of racehorses, Shadow noticed her backless dress skimmed her shoulder blades and dipped to just above the base of her spine. He was sure many men would find Her Grace alluring, but his first thought was that she could do with eating a decent meal. Perhaps he was getting old.

The library with its high, ornately moulded ceiling overlooked the castle gardens. Books lined every wall and a discreet wooden staircase led up to a balcony that ran around the room and gave access to the higher shelves. There were no windows, but French doors led out on to a terrace, and beyond there were perfectly manicured lawns and a huge pond with a fountain, the water shimmering in the sun. Peacocks omitted the occasional screech as they strutted along an avenue of stone statues.

Standing in front of a long mahogany table holding silver ice buckets and trays with various glasses and bottles of spirits, was an overweight, slightly balding man. He was dressed for dinner.

"These gentlemen are here to speak to you, Bertie. They are from the police," said the duchess before turning to leave. Shadow stepped forward.

"Good afternoon, Your Grace. My name is Chief Inspector Shadow and this is Sergeant Chang. We would like to ask you a few questions about what happened at the shoot this afternoon if we may?"

The duke turned around a cigar in one hand and a glass of what looked like whisky in the other.

"Extraordinary event! Absolute extraordinary! All started so well too. Should have been a cracking day. I've never known a shoot like it." He paused, raised his cigar to his lips and inhaled deeply. "Well, except for that time when Boozy

Carmichael's Lab stole his Purdey. Must have chased him over a furlong, poor old Boozy. Then of course last year, or was it the year before? Tubby Forbes-Hamilton brought that Russian chap, an oligarch apparently. Turned up in a white shirt. Well, I ask you? How did he ever expect to hit anything?"

Shadow glanced over to Jimmy. He wasn't entering anything into his ever-present electronic notebook.

"Why aren't you taking notes?" Shadow hissed at him, while the duke turned away to add more ice to his drink.

"I can't, Chief. I haven't got a clue what he's talking about," Jimmy hissed back while the duke continued to chatter on.

"Still never had a death before. Shame. Nice chap FitzAllan, and an absolute genius with the gee-gees, like one of those horse whispering fellows. You chaps found out what happened yet? Seems like a complete mystery to me."

"We can't be completely sure of anything at this stage and investigations are still ongoing," replied Shadow. "That's why we were hoping you might be able to help us."

"Darling," interrupted a voice behind them. Shadow looked around, slightly surprised to see that Annabel was standing by the door. Had she just returned, or did she never leave the room? "I was going to suggest these detectives return at a more appropriate time," she continued smoothly. "Our guests will be arriving shortly, and I don't want to shock them unnecessarily—it would ruin the evening. What happened today was unfortunate, but they are here to celebrate. It is the Glorious Twelfth after all."

"Quite right! Always have a bit of a do on the twelfth. Drinks and dinner this evening and a few are staying over too, a house party for the Ebor," the duke began to explain as he lit another cigar.

"Oh, darling, you really shouldn't. Remember what the doctor said," chided his wife.

"Now, Annabel, don't be a nag! The quack worked his magic; replaced the iffy valves. My ticker is as good as new," he replied, inhaling deeply once again.

"Dr Galbraith is hardly a quack, darling. There aren't any quacks on Harley Street."

"Ha!" barked the duke. "That's where you're wrong. You are impressed far too easily, Annabel. You think a chap is God, simply because he's been to university and got a few letters after his name. Binky Charlston's wife visited a chap on Harley Street, called himself a plastic surgeon. She came out looking like a waxwork. A melted one at that! Total mess! Speaking of which, I thought you were wearing the white dress this evening."

Except for a slight tightening of her jaw, Annabel didn't react to his insult.

"It was stained with wine from the last time I wore it. It had to be thrown out."

"Couldn't you have found something less funereal?" the duke grunted. "Mummy always says black is very ageing—

drains the colour—and I must say I agree with her."

"Don't you always," said Annabel under her breath, but her husband had turned to top up his drink. He didn't seem to hear her and continued talking.

"You could have gone out and bought a new frock. Lord knows what you've been doing all day. I hear poor Mummy even had to do the flowers for this evening."

Annabel opened her mouth to respond, but Shadow stepped in.

"I would still like to speak with the other members of today's shooting party," he insisted, before the conversation became more domesticated. Perhaps this is what happened when you were always surrounded by servants. You grew accustomed to private exchanges not being very private. "Sir Charles Richmond and Lord and Lady Eastwold, I believe."

"Naturally, Chief Inspector, but not today. After all you did say as yet you don't know if anyone else was involved in Mr FitzAllan's death. Perhaps it would be better if you left through the garden," suggested the duchess wearing a very brittle smile as she waved an elegant hand towards the open French doors. Shadow knew when he was being dismissed and suspected this instruction was close to being told to use the servants' entrance after all.

The two detectives stepped out of the library and on to the path of wide York flagstones that formed a terrace overlooking the impressive gardens. It was still very warm, but to the west the sun was slowly falling in the sky, casting a golden glow over the moors.

"Wow, this place is bigger than Museum Gardens and Dean's Park put together," said Jimmy as they made their way down the steps and on to a gravel path that ran between the lawns and down to the fountain. "How many gardeners do you think they have?"

"The more pressing question right now, Sergeant, is how do we get back to the car as the duchess has made it quite clear we are no longer welcome in the house?" replied Shadow looking around him. He had completely lost his bearings.

"Let's head towards the greenhouses, Chief," suggested Jimmy, pointing to the row of large red-brick and glass Victorian greenhouses, on the far right-hand side of the garden. "I'm sure we passed them driving in and one of the peacocks is heading over there, so I might be able to get a photo of him."

"Don't tell me," grumbled Shadow as they crunched along the gravel. "As well as a butler and a duke, you've never seen a peacock before either."

"Not in the wild."

"This isn't the wild, Sergeant."

"No, maybe not, Chief, but you know what I mean. I've been thinking I should learn more about wildlife. If I ever have children, I want to teach them about animals and stuff," said Jimmy as he took out his phone and began to click away. "The duke and duchess didn't seem very upset that one of guests had died, did they?"

"Like I said, that's the aristocracy for you," muttered Shadow as he noticed a lady stepping out of one of the greenhouses and walking towards them. She was average height, slim and wearing a simple cotton, floral-print dress. Her grey chin-length hair was covered by a wide-brimmed straw sun hat. A wax jacket similar to Shadow's was draped over her left arm and in her right hand she carried a large wooden trug piled high with poppies, foxgloves and other wildflowers. Shadow estimated that she was in her late seventies. Her face broke into a warm smile when she saw the two men.

"Let me guess. Lost ramblers? No, you aren't really dressed for a day yomping across the moors. Men from the ministry? No, you don't look like civil servants either and it's a little late for you to be working."

Shadow shook his head as he held out his hand.

"I'm afraid not. We're the police. Chief Inspector Shadow and Sergeant Chang," he replied. The older lady's smile faded as she placed the trug carefully on the ground and returned his handshake.

"Then you must be here regarding the death of the poor Irish gentleman. I'm Sybil DeVere by the way."

"Did you know Mr FitzAllan?" asked Jimmy.

"Yes, I knew him. He trained my son's horses and before that, my late husband's."

"Were you involved with today's shoot at all?" asked

Shadow before Jimmy could jump in again. Sybil's smile returned, but she shook her head.

"No, Chief Inspector, I'm afraid my shooting days are over. Anyway, I hear it was very much a boys' day out, although I'm sure Lavinia tagged along too. She does hate to think she's missing out."

"Who's Lavinia?" enquired Jimmy, who had swapped his phone for his electronic notebook and had begun tapping away again.

"Lavinia Eastwold, my son's sister-in-law."

Jimmy frowned, clearly struggling to keep track of the family dynamics. At the same time one of the castle's gardeners walked by wearing a flat cap and carrying a spade over his shoulder.

"Good evening, Your Grace, gentlemen," he said nodding in their direction and raising his hand to touch his cap. "Let me take care of these for you, Your Grace," he said, picking up the trug and continuing on his way.

"Evening, Bill, and thank you," Sybil replied.

"If you are the duke's mother, does that make you a duchess too?" Jimmy asked, looking a little embarrassed.

"I became the dowager duchess following the death of my husband—Xander—and before my marriage I was the Honourable Sybil Davenport. I appreciate your confusion, Sergeant, but please call me Sybil. First names make life so much simpler. Now if you will excuse me, we're having a party this evening and I must change. Would you gentlemen care to join us? I'm sure you must be hungry and thirsty."

"That's very kind, but I'm not entirely sure we would be welcome," said Shadow.

Sybil gave a knowing nod of her head.

"Ah I see, then you must have already met Annabel, my daughter-in-law." She paused and studied the chief inspector. "You said your name was Shadow. Many years ago we had tenants with that name. Jack and Elsie Shadow at Church Farm. Are you any relation?"

"Yes, they were my grandparents," replied Shadow.

"Then you must be the son of Constable Shadow." And the older lady's smile faded once again. "I remember what happened that night. It was a tragedy for your family, and you were only a little boy. I'm so very sorry." She seemed lost in her thoughts for a moment, then her tone became more businesslike. "Now I expect you are trying to locate your car. If you walk through that door to you right," she said pointing to a small wooden door set into the garden wall, "you will find yourself in the walled garden, where we grow all our own vegetables, although it's a constant battle with the damn rabbits. There's another door on the far side wall. Go through that and you'll arrive on the west lawn. You should be able to see your car from there."

The detectives thanked her and followed her directions, which indeed led them back to their car. As they were leaving, they saw several Range Rovers and at least one Bentley arrive.

"It would be worth staying just to see all the flash cars," said Jimmy as he tried to discreetly photograph a vintage Aston Martin gliding by. They drove back down the long driveway and turned right at the gatehouse towards the village. Shadow noticed the lace curtains hanging in one of the gatehouse windows twitch as they passed by. He turned to look and see who was there, but he suddenly heard a horn blare, and Jimmy slammed on the brakes. Shadow's head jerked awkwardly.

"For crying out loud. What are you doing?" he demanded, rubbing his sore neck.

"Sorry, Chief, that horsebox came round the corner really quickly," Jimmy explained gesturing towards the vehicle that was now racing towards the village. "Do you want me to follow it?"

"No forget about it, but look where you're going from now on," grumbled Shadow.

As they drove back through the village, they came to the pub, the DeVere Arms, and Shadow spotted a Land Rover parked outside with a spaniel and two Labradors hanging their heads out of the back window. It was still warm and the late evening sun was reflecting off the pub windows. Two young men in checked shirts and tweed breeks were sitting outside at one of the wooden picnic tables. They had rolled up their sleeves and removed their ties.

"Pull over here," Shadow ordered. "These two look like they've been shooting. Let's call in for a quick drink." Jimmy parked next to the Land Rover, and the dogs greeted them with a loud chorus of woofs and howls.

"Quiet!" ordered one of the young men firmly and the dogs immediately fell silent. A middle-aged woman came bustling out of the pub carrying two glass tumblers of dark liquid on a tray. Her hair was an unnatural shade of red and she was wearing a low-cut, clingy leopard-print top with her tight jeans and high heels. She placed the two glasses down in front of the young men.

"Brandy! That's what you need for shock," she declared, "on the house of course, my loves."

"Thanks, Bet," replied the young man with his back to Shadow and Jimmy as he took a grateful sip.

"I can't, Bet, I'm driving," protested the other young man who had silenced the dogs.

"Don't be daft, Giles. Leave the Landy where it is. You only live across the road," replied the barmaid, who they now knew was called Bet. Shadow's eyes followed her hand with the fingernails painted exactly the same shade as her hair as she pointed to the little cottage where he'd been born. There was a single-storey extension to the side of the cottage that was now a garage but had once been the tiny village police station. All Shadow could remember about the place was a strong smell of furniture polish and the large brass bell on the counter, which he had sometimes been allowed to play with. Still, it felt strange to think of this young man living there. He had somehow imagined it would be frozen in time.

He was so deep in thought that at first he didn't notice Bet, the barmaid, had spoken and was staring at him expectantly. Jimmy nudged him with his elbow.

"I'm sorry," said Shadow with a start, "did you say something?"

"I said, what can I get you, love?" repeated the barmaid, her hands firmly placed on her hips as she looked him up and down with an expert eye.

"A pint of Black Sheep please and a mineral water for my sergeant," said Shadow without thinking. Bet's heavily pencilled eyebrows shot up.

"Police are you? I should have guessed. Well, you certainly didn't waste any time. Poor Flynn—the village won't be the same without him. Good-looking too, a bit like a younger version of yourself. I've always had a thing for coppers. Now take a seat and don't be upsetting Giles and Fred with your questions. They've had a nasty shock," she ordered before disappearing back into the pub with a little wiggle of her hips and leaving behind an embarrassed Shadow and Jimmy, who couldn't stop grinning.

"I think you've pulled, Chief," he whispered.

"Oh, shut up," snapped Shadow, then cleared his throat and approached the two young men, who were now looking a little wary as they continued to sip their brandies. "Excuse me, gentlemen, my name is Chief Inspector Shadow and this is Sergeant Chang. May we ask you a few questions?"

The young man Bet had addressed as Giles stood up and

politely held out his hand. "Of course. I'm Giles Green-wood. I found Flynn's body."

His companion followed suit.

"Fred Houlston. I was loader for Sir Charles today." Shadow and Jimmy sat down opposite the two young men on the wooden bench.

"Can you tell me what happened today?" asked Shadow.

"It was just a normal day. I was the loader for Lord East-wold, but His Grace was getting tired of waiting for Mr FitzAllan to return from his phone call, so Dad sent me to look for him," replied Giles.

"Had the shoot stopped for Mr FitzAllan's phone call?"

"No, not exactly. We'd had lunch in the old chapel. There's always a table and chairs set up in there on shoot days, so we can eat in the shade and the food doesn't get spoilt in the sun. We bring a hamper with us from the castle kitchens you see," Giles explained. "We'd finished eating and were heading back when Flynn's phone rang. He went to answer it in the copse, and we went back to the butts."

"Why didn't he answer it and keep walking with the rest of you?" asked Jimmy.

Giles shrugged.

"The signal is better in the copse I guess, or maybe he wanted some privacy."

"Was there anyone else nearby when you found Mr FitzAllan?" asked Shadow.

"No, everyone was up on the moor."

Shadow turned his attention to Fred. "You said you were Sir Charles's loader. Who was Mr FitzAllan's loader?"

"He didn't have one. He only had a single gun, you see. The other gentlemen each had a pair. The loader loads the gun they aren't using to save time. Wilf was Lady Eastwold's loader and Rory was with His Grace."

"Where are they now?" asked Shadow.

"They went home. They both live on farms up on the moors. I don't think either of them saw much. As soon as Dad saw the body, he told them to keep the dogs away, so they didn't disturb anything," explained Giles.

"We believe the pellets that killed Mr FitzAllan were quite small in size. Does that mean anything to either of you?"

"The cartridges Mr FitzAllan used would have the smallest pellets," replied Fred. "His gun is a twenty-gauge, the others were all using twelve-gauge guns."

Shadow nodded as the young man confirmed what Ben and Ollie had said.

"How did he seem to you?"

The two young men exchanged a glance.

"Same as always," said Giles.

"In a good mood," added Fred. "He was having a decent day, probably hit more birds than anyone else despite only having the one gun. Why? Do you think he might have killed himself?"

"We are still making inquiries," replied Shadow smoothly. "Would you say he was popular generally within the village? Did he have any enemies that you know of?"

"No, he was a nice guy. Generous, always tipped well after a shoot," said Giles.

"Better than Eastwold," muttered Fred into his pint.

"My girlfriend Clancy works for him. She says he's a great boss," added Giles.

"The ladies certainly seemed to like him," agreed Fred.

At that moment, Bet returned with their drinks and placed them down on the table.

"Thank you," said Shadow, careful not to make eye contact.

"Will you be eating with us too? There's a free table inside and we've got some lovely lamb chops on as a special tonight," she asked. Shadow's mouth began to water. He was torn between his growling stomach and wanting to avoid the slightly terrifying Bet. Jimmy stood up with a knowing look.

"I'll ring Sophie and let her know I won't be back for a while, Chief," he said.

Shadow picked up their drinks, thanked Fred and Giles, followed Bet inside and took a seat at the table by the window. He inhaled the appealing aroma unique to a country pub: a perfect combination of hand-pulled beer, home-cooked food and a hint of damp dog. It was busy inside with most tables taken and a group of older farmers in flat caps standing at the bar. He couldn't help noticing there was a slight lull in people's conversations when he made his entrance. In one corner, huddled together, were some of the young grooms from FitzAllan's stables. They were all drinking pints of Guinness and at least two were still dabbing their eyes with tissues.

Out of the corner of his eye, Shadow could see Bet bearing down on him with two menus in her hand and he felt a great sense of relief when at that moment Jimmy entered the pub and intercepted her. He was unusually quiet as he sat down and handed over a menu.

"Anything wrong?" asked Shadow as he took a long grateful drink of his beer.

"Not really, but Sophie wasn't answering her phone, so I had to leave her a message," explained Jimmy looking a little worried as he took his seat opposite Shadow.

"Maybe she's out on a call," suggested Shadow, who was now only half listening as he read the menu and considered the other specials that were chalked up on the blackboard behind the bar. He decided on the lamb chops and sent Jimmy to place their order before Bet could make another appearance. Then nodded as his sergeant gestured that he was going outside to try phoning Sophie again. Through the window, Shadow watched as Clancy arrived and wrapped her arms around Giles. The two of them waved goodbye to Fred, then released the dogs from the Land Rover and made their way across the road to their cottage. He looked around the pub and wondered how different his life could have been if his father had lived and they'd stayed in the village. Would the people drinking here tonight be his friends? Would he belong rather than feel like an outsider, treated with suspicion? Jimmy returned looking much happier.

"It's okay, Chief, she'd left me a message saying she missed me because she was trying to talk to Donaldson. She is on call tonight, but I think she was hoping he might let her observe his post-mortem."

"Well, I can't fault her optimism," replied Shadow, settling back in his chair, while Jimmy scrolled through the photos on his phone of the village and surrounding countryside.

"Don't you think it would be great to raise a family around here, Chief?"

Shadow raised an eyebrow. "That's the second time you've mentioned becoming a father. Is there something you want to tell me, Sergeant?"

Jimmy looked puzzled, then flushed in embarrassment. "Oh no, nothing like that, Chief. We want to get married before we think about having children. I was only planning ahead. It would be great if we could have one of each, you know a boy and girl, and we could take them on long country walks and bike rides. I could teach them how to fish and we could get a puppy."

"Do you know how to fish?" interrupted Shadow in surprise. This was a talent his sergeant had so far remained uncharacteristically quiet about.

Jimmy shifted in his seat. "Well, no," he admitted, "but

that's what I meant—living out here it's the sort of thing you could learn."

Shadow shook his head and took another sip of his pint. "Well, I'm certainly not an expert in these matters, but you might want to run all these ideas past Sophie before you make too many plans."

"Oh, Sophie will be great at all that. She'll be an amazing mum."

At that moment, Bet appeared with their food. "Aren't you going to interrogate me?" she asked placing the plates down in front of them with a flourish.

"Not unless you can think of anyone who might wish Mr FitzAllan harm?" replied Shadow as he placed the paper napkin on his knee.

Bet crossed her arms over her ample chest and wrinkled her noise. "No, Flynn was a lovely man. I never once heard him raise his voice, not like that wife of his. Even when Plum was once in here haranguing him about horse racing being cruel, he always kept his cool."

"Plum?" queried Shadow.

"Lady Victoria DeVere, the duke's sister. Everyone calls her Plum," explained Bet.

"I see, well thank you for the information," said Shadow, hoping she would leave now, so he could enjoy his chops in peace.

"Always happy to help, Handsome." She gave him a wink before wiggling off again. Shadow picked up his knife and fork, ignoring the sniggering coming from Jimmy's direction.

ABOUT AN HOUR later, they left the pub and returned to their car. With a stomach full of lamb chops, new potatoes and beer, Shadow was looking forward to a snooze on his way home, but his sergeant, who seemed allergic to silence, cleared his throat ominously.

"I hope you didn't think I was being tactless, Chief," he said.

"You? Never?"

"When I mentioned raising a family here, after what Sybil said back at the castle. I didn't want to say anything in the pub, but I was going to ask you about what happened to your father?" asked Jimmy, who had also lost his father when he was young. "I know he died when you were only a kid. Did he really live here?"

"Yes, he was the constable in Kirkdale, back in the days when every village had its own police station. We lived in Giles's cottage," said Shadow, pointing across the road. "One evening he went to investigate reports of poachers on the estate, and he was shot dead. His killer was never found."

"Wow," replied Jimmy looking shocked. "So you really are a local! You've never mentioned him before. Don't you like talking about it?"

"No."

They sat in an awkward silence for a few moments.

Finally, Jimmy spoke again. "I was wondering, why isn't the plural of grouse grice, you know like mouse and mice, Chief?" he asked.

Shadow sighed and closed his eyes. It was going to be a long drive back to York.

CHAPTER THREE

Across 1. The upper class to the coast I carry (11 letters)

HIS PREDICTION WAS correct. Thanks to the tractors working late to bring in the harvest, and Shadow's insistence that Jimmy didn't overtake them on the narrow lanes, it was almost eleven o'clock when they arrived back at the station. As the two detectives walked through the reception area, Shadow sensed something was wrong. There was a subdued air about the place.

"What's going on?" he asked Tom, the constable who was manning the front desk.

"It's Sergeant Hedley, sir. He's been arrested on suspicion of causing death by dangerous driving," replied Tom whose young face was white with concern.

"What?" asked Shadow in astonishment. Sergeant George Hedley was in charge of the records office. He was the station's longest-serving officer and one of the few people Shadow could call a friend.

"He's downstairs in the custody suite, sir," explained Tom. Shadow hurried down the stone steps to what had once been the cellars of the medieval guildhall. He marched

48

straight up to the custody desk.

"Tom tells me you are holding George down here," he began angrily, but the custody sergeant held up his hands as if to defend himself.

"None of us wanted to, Chief, but the chief constable insisted."

Shadow paused. Chief Constable Maxwell was usually based in Northallerton at the North Yorkshire Police Headquarters.

"What on earth was she doing here?" he asked.

"Well, she arrived early this evening. She wanted a tour of the station. Apparently, she's interviewing applicants to replace Superintendent Branston and wanted to familiarise herself with the place."

Shadow snorted. Familiarise herself? He couldn't recall her ever visiting the station before. Superintendent Branston had taken unexpected early retirement a few weeks ago, due to his wife's ill health. Shadow and Branston had maintained an excellent working relationship over the years, achieved largely by staying out of each other's way. He had a feeling the equitable balance between uniform and CID wouldn't last long if Branston's successor was appointed by the chief constable.

"Anyway," continued the custody sergeant, "she heard about the shooting up at Kirkdale, so she seemed keen to hang around, then we got the call about George. We'd have let him go home while we investigated, but she insisted we follow proper procedure. I didn't want to keep him in, Chief."

Shadow nodded. It was clearly not the custody sergeant's fault.

"All right, I'll go and talk to him. Where is he? You haven't locked him up, have you?" he asked as the sound of one of the regular drunks singing echoed out of the cell closest to them.

"Of course not, Chief," replied the custody sergeant looking hurt. "He's waiting in the meeting room."

Shadow was relieved George wasn't in a cell or one of the interview rooms. The meeting room was a less formal space used to speak to vulnerable witnesses or grieving relatives. He opened the door and found his friend looking forlorn as he sat alone on one of the sofas. George's face was pale and worried when he stood up to greet Shadow. He was wearing an open-necked shirt and chinos. Somehow, Shadow thought he looked older out of his uniform.

"What happened?" he asked pulling a chair close to his old friend and sitting down next to him.

George shook his head slowly. "I just was driving home, John. Carol and I had been babysitting for Harry while his mum and dad went out for a meal. It's their anniversary, you see. Anyway, I was driving past the Knavesmire, opposite the Lucky Horseshoe. I was doing less than thirty, and a fox darted out from nowhere. I swerved and hit what I thought was a pile of black bin bags on the edge of the road—you know, left out for the dustbin lorry—but it turned out there was someone lying in the middle of them. I knew something was wrong the second I hit him, but I didn't see him, and I swear I hadn't been drinking."

"Of course you hadn't. Who said you had?" demanded Shadow, furious on his friend's behalf.

"They had to breathalyse me and take a blood sample. It's procedure—you know that. The chief constable was here. She said if there was an inquiry or a criminal case to answer, we couldn't be seen to have acted inappropriately because a fellow officer was involved."

George's voice caught on the words *criminal case*. Shadow reached out and placed a hand on the shoulder of his older colleague.

"Look, try not to worry. Where's Carol now? Does she know what's going on?"

"Yes, I called her. She wanted to come down here with me, but I told her to go home. Tom drove her back. I was frightened I might get put in cuffs and I couldn't have let her see me like that."

"They didn't did they?" Shadow was feeling more and more outraged by the second. It was one thing to show impartiality, but didn't over thirty years' service count for anything?

"No, no, everyone has been very understanding but I was so shaken up I didn't know what was going to happen."

"I'll go and get you a fresh cup of tea and see if we can

get you out of here. Have you spoken to a solicitor or a union rep?"

George looked startled. "You don't think it will come to that do you, John? I thought they'd get the test results back and I could go home."

Shadow stood up and patted George on the shoulder again.

"You're probably right. I'll go and chase up the lab, see what's taking so long. I'll be back as soon as I can."

WHEN SHADOW STEPPED out of the meeting room, he found Jimmy waiting for him.

"How is he, Chief?"

"How do you think?" snapped Shadow, his anger at George's treatment was making him even more irritable than usual. "Find out where his test results are and what's happening with the post-mortem on the man he hit. Then get someone to bring him a cup of tea."

"I'm already on it, Chief," replied Jimmy as he began tapping numbers into his mobile phone, "and I've told Sophie we'll meet her at the mortuary."

For the first time that day, Shadow was relieved that Sophie hadn't been called to the shooting incident, and that she was on duty now instead. He very much doubted Donaldson would have dealt with tonight's victim so quickly.

However, his relief, was short-lived when half an hour later, he saw Sophie's worried expression. They found her at the washroom of the mortuary removing her protective clothing and washing her hands, having just completed the post-mortem.

"Not good news I'm afraid, Chief," she said. "The victim was still alive when George hit him. He had been struck on the head with a blunt object. It had fractured his skull and there was a lot of bleeding in the brain. Had he been left there he would probably have died of his injuries, but he was unconscious, not dead when George's car hit him. The impact caused twelve rib fractures and…" She glanced up at Shadow who was turning pale. She knew he was notoriously squeamish. "Well, let's just say there were multiple internal injuries. I'm sorry it's not better news."

"It's not your fault, Sophie. Anything else? Any sign he'd been involved in a fight?"

"No, I don't think so. There aren't any bruises or abrasions to his knuckles or anywhere else on his body."

"Had he taken anything?"

"No drugs, but alcohol levels in his blood were very high, the equivalent of being four times over the drink drive limit."

"That fits in with what the landlord at the Lucky Horseshoe told uniform, Chief," added Jimmy. "He said the victim had been drinking in there for hours."

"So could he have passed out from the alcohol and then hit his head or was he definitely hit by something?" asked

53

Shadow, wondering if there was any way his death could be ruled as misadventure by the coroner. Sophie shook her head.

"No, he received a pretty hefty blow to the back of the skull. I need to do a few more tests, but I would say he was hit by something metal, not too big and slightly curved. I would also say whoever hit him was taller than him, but then he is only five foot three."

Shadow turned to Jimmy.

"Find out if anything fitting that description was found at the crime scene—anything, even if it might not seem like an obvious weapon, like say an old-fashioned dustbin lid. Make sure any CCTV in the area is checked too, not only the one at the pub. Tell them not to overlook anything. I don't want George's life to be ruined because we missed something. Then I suppose we should concentrate on identifying the victim."

"Actually, Chief, identification won't be a problem, but it has made the whole thing a lot more complicated," said Jimmy, who was simultaneously making notes on his electronic notepad while trying to read the messages coming through on his phone. "The victim still had his wallet on him, so it was easy to identify him. His name is Aidan O'Doyle and he's the head stable lad for Flynn FitzAllan. Although, lad is stretching it a bit—he was fifty-eight."

Shadow stared at his sergeant for a moment.

"Are you telling me that a famous racehorse trainer and

the man in charge of running his stables died within a few hours of each other and their deaths are…let's say suspicious at the very least?"

"I take it you don't think it's a coincidence then, Chief?" asked Jimmy, earning himself a scowl. Sophie was looking a little happier though.

"If it isn't a coincidence and they were both targeted by the same person, surely that would be good for George," she suggested. Shadow sighed. He wasn't so confident. The Crown Prosecution Service often moved in mysterious ways.

"What else did they find in his pockets?" he asked.

"Other than his wallet, which still had all his bank cards and some cash in it, only his mobile. Forensics have them both," said Jimmy scrolling through the information he'd been sent. "They are running tests, but Ben has read the last text message he received. It was sent at ten thirty and it said, 'Meet me outside,' and was in response to a text the victim sent a couple of hours earlier."

"And what did that say?" asked Shadow, unable to hide his impatience.

"'Ten grand to shut me up,'" replied Jimmy.

Shadow raised his eyebrows. "So, Aidan was blackmailing someone, or someone was bribing him, and it looks like they found a cheaper way to guarantee his silence. Can we trace the other mobile?"

"Forensics are on it, Chief."

"Who's his next of kin?"

"Well, he's an Irish national, like FitzAllan, so it hasn't been easy. We haven't contacted the stables yet, but we think Tom has managed to track down a brother living in Cork through social media."

"Get Tom to contact the Irish police tomorrow to check, then ask them to inform the brother and see if they can find any more information about Aidan."

Jimmy's phone bleeped.

"George's test results have come back negative," he said with a relieved smile.

"There should never have been any doubt that they wouldn't," grunted Shadow.

"If Aidan was hit over the head because he was black-mailing someone, what does that mean for George?" asked Sophie.

"In the short term, it means I'm going back to the station to sign his release papers. He's been there too long as it is."

Jimmy and Sophie exchanged a concerned look.

"What about the chief constable?" asked his sergeant.

Shadow shrugged. "I'll worry about her in the morning."

THE MINSTER BELLS were striking two when Shadow finally arrived home. He lived alone on *Florence*, a narrow boat moored on the River Ouse by Skeldergate Bridge. She had been his home for almost thirty years. He'd bought her when he'd first served as a constable in London, before returning to his home city of York, after the death of Luisa—his girlfriend. His stomach grumbled loudly as he kicked off his shoes and shrugged off his jacket. It had been a long day and the upset with George had done nothing to aid his digestion. After a quick rummage through the cupboards of his compact galley he found a half-empty packet of tablets to help settle the churning. He popped a couple in his mouth and let them dissolve before falling into bed and an uneasy sleep.

Despite his late night, Shadow was awake early the next morning. The previous day's events were occupying his mind too much to allow more than a few hours of sleep. He showered and dressed quickly, but his fridge and cupboards were so bare he couldn't even make a cup of coffee. The sun was glistening on the water and it was already warm when he stepped on to the towpath. His neighbours the geese were awake early too and honking loudly at any joggers and dog walkers who got too close.

It was too early for Bettys to be open for breakfast, so instead he took a bag of dirty washing straight to the laundry he used on Goodramgate. Although there was a washing machine on board *Florence*, Shadow preferred to have his suits and shirts cleaned professionally. The laundry was owned by Maggie, an old friend from his primary school days. Despite the early hour, she didn't look particularly surprised to see him, nor did she mince her words.

"You look terrible. Didn't you get enough sleep? What

was keeping you awake? This awful business with poor old George or is there more to Flynn FitzAllan's death than meets the eye?"

Shadow was no longer surprised that Maggie already knew about everything that was going on. Thanks to her extensive network of friends, family and her ability to chat to everyone she met, she was possibly York's most well-informed resident.

"A little of both," he replied with a sigh as he dumped his laundry bag on her counter.

"So, was it a case of foul play with Flynn? A jealous lover perhaps?" she pressed on with a mischievous grin. Shadow gave her a reproachful look. She knew perfectly well he couldn't discuss the details of any case, but she just gave him an innocent smile in return.

A thought occurred to Shadow. "Have you heard something or was that a guess?" he asked.

"An educated guess maybe," replied Maggie as she began to sort through his shirts and fill out a receipt. "Flynn FitzAllan was in here about a week ago with a shirt and jacket he wanted me to get a red wine stain out of, telling me some blarney about how he'd got overexcited watching a horse of his win at Ripon and spilt it on himself."

"What makes you think it was blarney?"

Maggie pursed her lips and gave Shadow a knowing look.

"Picture it—if you spill wine on yourself it goes on the front of your shirt and jacket, but his were stained on the back and shoulders too, like someone had poured a glass of wine over his head. Now in my experience, men don't tend to throw wine over someone when they are angry, but women do. Women who have been wronged."

"It sounds like you are speaking from personal experience."

"I may have chucked the odd glass of Merlot in my time," she replied, her dark eyes twinkling a little, "but in my defence I was always provoked."

"You're sure it was FitzAllan?"

"Of course." She pointed to the copy of the *Racing Post* lying on the counter. "I like a flutter every now and again. Flynn FitzAllan was quite the rising star. His horses are always getting tipped. I backed his last two winners and made a tidy profit. You can take that if you want. I've already picked my runners for today."

Shadow picked up the newspaper. The front page was dedicated to Flynn's obituary and was accompanied by a photograph of him with one of his horses winning at Newmarket only a few weeks ago. It felt strange to see his face smiling and full of joy compared to how he'd seen it yesterday—damaged and lifeless. Shadow conceded that Flynn had been a handsome man with high cheekbones, bright blue eyes and his dark hair worn in a style that Shadow thought was a little too long and effeminate, but he understood some women might find attractive.

After leaving Maggie, Shadow went straight to Bettys

Tearooms on St Helen's Square and arrived as they were opening their doors. He was more ready than ever for his full English with a pot of Yorkshire tea and took his usual seat in the corner of the room. He opened his copy of the *Yorkshire Post*, noting that their lead story was also the death of Flynn, before turning his attention to the crossword. By the time he'd swallowed his last mouthful of bacon, there was only one clue remaining. He tapped his pen against the table as he tried to solve it, but his concentration was interrupted by another tapping sound and a sense he was being watched. He looked up and sure enough there was Jimmy's finger tapping the glass and his face smiling at him through the window. Having got his attention, his sergeant then began an elaborate mime of pointing to his watch, then back towards the police station, pulling an angry face, then drawing a finger across his neck before finishing with a thumbs up. Shadow sighed as he stood and pulled on his coat. He supposed he should be grateful that he'd at least managed to finish eating in peace.

"Good morning, Sergeant. Are you planning on becoming a Marcel Marceau tribute act or do you have something to tell me that couldn't wait until I arrived at the station?" he asked as he stepped out into St Helen's Square.

"A couple of things actually, Chief," replied Jimmy cheerfully ignoring Shadow's sarcastic tone. "Firstly, Dr Donaldson has the results of the post-mortem on Flynn FitzAllan, but as usual he's only willing to discuss them with you."

"At least he isn't insisting on sharing them with the duke first," grunted Shadow. "What else?"

"The chief constable wants to speak to you too."

"Okay, I'll phone her after I've spoken to Donaldson."

"Actually, Chief, you'll be able to speak to her in person. She's at the station and I got the impression she isn't very happy."

Shadow groaned. Their relationship was difficult enough when the chief constable was in Northallerton and they were separated by a distance of thirty miles. He couldn't see it improving when they were both in the same building.

Back at the station, Shadow went straight to his office to call Donaldson. Waiting on his desk was a copy of *Debrett's Peerage* that he had asked Tom to find for him before he'd left last night. He hoped it might help him understand the dynamics of the DeVere family. He laid Maggie's copy of the *Racing Post* alongside the hefty reference book. Then he picked up the telephone receiver with a sigh and dialled the number for Donaldson. The call was answered by Miss Habbershaw, the dragon in human form who fiercely guarded access to the doctor.

"I'm sorry, Chief Inspector," she began, not sounding remotely sorry, "Dr Donaldson tried calling you earlier, but he is now too busy to speak with you. I am, however, in the process of typing the report for your case and it should be with you in the next day or two."

Shadow's jaw tightened. This was typical of Donaldson's pettiness. Making himself unavailable simply because Shadow had missed his call. Two days was far too long to wait.

"Thank you, Miss Habbershaw, but it would be helpful if you could provide me with the answer to two questions now," replied Shadow, trying to keep the impatience out of his voice. "I really do need to know the size of the pellets found in the victim and whether he was definitely shot first in the back, not in the head."

"Hold the line a moment please, Chief Inspector, and I'll see if Dr Donaldson will permit me to reveal that information," said Miss Habbershaw primly. Shadow waited as the phone went quiet and watched as the minute hand on the wall clock ticked around the face fully five times before she returned.

"Chief Inspector? Dr Donaldson has kindly allowed me to inform you that the lead pellets were three millimetres in size and that the victim was hit first in the back and then in the head, as he suspected."

Shadow managed to stop himself asking why if she could speak to Donaldson directly he hadn't been able to, and instead thanked her and hung up. Now for the next difficult conversation.

THE CHIEF CONSTABLE had temporarily taken over Superintendent Branston's office on the ground floor. Shadow couldn't remember the last time he'd been there. Although Branston was the superior officer at the station, he knew he had risen as high as he could hope for and was quite happy to spend his last few working years quietly watering the plants in his office until the day of his retirement. Shadow doubted whoever the chief constable chose to replace Branston would be quite so easy-going. He didn't know why she couldn't just promote Deputy Superintendent Clarkson. He was responsible for the day-to-day running of the uniform division and left Shadow and CID to their own devices. With an impending sense of doom, Shadow knocked on the office door and waited.

"Come in," said an all too familiar, slightly shrill voice. Shadow opened the door and stepped inside. The place felt strangely empty without Branston's vast collection of plants, but the scent of tobacco from his pipe still lingered. The chief constable was sitting at Branston's old desk. She was a slim, athletic woman of medium height, who wore her grey hair cropped short. Her face was free of any trace of make-up and her blue eyes had deep creases in the corners, which Shadow found quite odd as he struggled to recall her ever smiling.

"You've had quite an eventful twenty-four hours, I understand, Shadow," she said by way of a greeting.

"Yes, ma'am," replied Shadow.

"Two unexplained deaths, one involving a fellow officer."

"Yes, ma'am," repeated Shadow, not sure why she had called him in only to tell him what he already knew.

"I hope I don't need to remind you that proper procedure must be followed. From the evidence I have seen it looks like Sergeant Hedley could be facing a charge of causing death by dangerous driving, yet I see you released him from custody last night. We must not be shown to be giving Sergeant Hedley any preferential treatment just because of our own personal regard for him."

"No, ma'am," said Shadow, although he doubted the chief constable had any personal regard for George or even knew his first name until yesterday, despite him being the longest-serving officer in the station.

"The other death, the shooting, will also need to be treated extremely carefully, Shadow. Many of those involved are prominent figures in the county."

Now Shadow knew what the meeting was about. The chief constable was more worried he was going to upset the duke and his friends than about the future of one of her officers.

"Sir Charles Richmond has already telephoned me," she continued. "Since the story broke overnight the press have descended on Kirkdale. I have sent several uniformed officers from Thirsk to the entrance of both Mr FitzAllan's stables and Kirkdale Castle to prevent any harassment. I understand you plan to return to the village today and would ask you to avoid any interaction with the press too."

"Yes, ma'am. On the subject of Sergeant Hedley… We believe there is a connection between the death of the victim in his case—Aidan O'Doyle—and Mr FitzAllan. The two men worked together and died on the same day. If we can prove the blow to Mr O'Doyle's head was attempted murder, would that have implications for the case against Sergeant Hedley?"

The chief constable put the pen she'd been holding down and laced her fingers together, resting her chin on them as she considered what he was asking before responding.

"Yes, Shadow, I think if you could prove a more serious crime had been committed against Mr O'Doyle that would cast quite a different light on Sergeant Hedley's situation."

"Thank you, ma'am," replied Shadow, as she dismissed him with a wave of her hand.

TEN MINUTES AND several phone calls later, Shadow was relieved to be finally getting out of the station and the city for the day. He wanted to put as much distance as possible between himself and the chief constable, even if it did mean enduring Jimmy's driving and chatter.

"Sophie liked all the photos I took, but I couldn't convince her that we should move out to the countryside. She said as we both have jobs that need us to be on call, we should probably stay in York."

"Yes, well she does have a point." Shadow sighed. Thankfully, Sophie was far more pragmatic than her fiancé. "What have you got there?" he asked pointing to another book wedged at an angle into the compartment between them that usually held Jimmy's takeaway coffees.

"It's a pocket guide to British wildlife. I thought, you know, while we were out in the countryside, I could tick off anything new I see. There's a section in the back for trees and flowers as well. Is this the right time of year for blue-bells? They're Sophie's favourites."

"No," replied Shadow. He had brought reading material of his own: the racing newspaper and *Debrett's* and if Jimmy shut up long enough, he might actually be able to find something useful in them before they arrived in Kirkdale.

"Oh, look what's that? Is it a lady pheasant?" asked Jimmy suddenly as he swerved and narrowly missed a bird that had run out in front of them.

"No, it's a partridge," growled Shadow, putting his hand against the dashboard to steady himself as the *Racing Post* fell on to the floor. "And for crying out loud, look where you're going."

"Excellent, I haven't got one of those. Sorry, Chief."

After narrowly missing two more of the county's game birds, Jimmy's phone began to bleep. He glanced at the screen.

"It's a message from forensics, Chief," he said.

"Then stop in this gateway and see what they have to say," ordered Shadow, grateful for a pause in the erratic swerving and braking. Jimmy pulled over and picked up his phone and began reading the text.

"They are liaising with Donaldson about the pellets found in Flynn; apparently there is an anomaly with those in the cartridges he was using at the shoot. The ones Donaldson removed were made of lead, but ones Flynn used, at least the ones they found in his pocket, contained steel shot. They've checked his burner phone and it only ever received calls and messages from one number, until yesterday when he got a message from a new number. They've managed to fix the smashed phone and around the time of his death he received a message from the number that usually called the burner."

"What were these two messages? Who were they from?" asked Shadow who was struggling to make sense of what he was being told.

"They don't say, but they are going to get all the texts transcribed." Jimmy paused and smiled. "They say the messages on the burner are definitely from a woman and some of the stuff is quite sweet! I wonder if it was from his wife—maybe they had a good relationship after all."

Shadow, however, remained unimpressed.

"Why didn't Ben and Ollie call us with all this? They've left out half the information we need. Call them back."

"Sorry, I can't, Chief," apologised Jimmy. "The signal

here isn't strong enough. It looks like they tried phoning us but couldn't get through. The signal is pretty hit and miss."

Shadow tutted and shook his head. What was the point of all this high-tech equipment if it didn't work when you wanted it to?

"We'll have to try them again later." He sighed. "Let's get going."

When they set off again, Shadow relayed to his sergeant the news Maggie had shared with him about Flynn and the wine-stained clothing.

"So do you think he was having an affair, Chief?"

"Well, all the evidence seems to be pointing in that direction. First Maggie's story and then this business with the burner phone. Despite your optimism, Sergeant, I don't know why any man would need an untraceable phone to contact his own wife."

Jimmy's face fell.

"Oh, I hope he wasn't having a fling with Clancy. I saw her leaving the pub with Giles last night and thought they made a really cute couple."

Shadow shook his head at his sergeant's sentimentality and returned to his reading material.

CHAPTER FOUR

Across 5. Ride the filly or stallion along the shore (5 letters)

B EFORE LEAVING THE station, Shadow had telephoned both FitzAllan's stables and Kirkdale Castle. Clancy sounded like she had been crying again and said that they had only just heard about Aidan. She told him Siobhan FitzAllan would be leaving for the racecourse at around half past eleven. Jarvis informed him that the duke was holding a small luncheon party before also departing for the races, so they decided to head for the Grange first. As the chief constable had warned, journalists and camera crews were gathered at the entrance, but the uniformed officers from Thirsk waved Shadow's car through. Clancy was there to greet them when they arrived. She looked a little flustered and out of breath.

"Hello there, I thought I was going to miss you. I nipped into the church and lit another candle for poor old Aidan. It's not a Catholic church of course—my mother would never forgive me—but it will have to do for now. And I had to go the long way around to avoid that nosy lot," she said gesturing to the press in the distance.

The two detectives followed Clancy back around the house to the stable yard. They were met with a far more chaotic scene than the previous day and unlike yesterday, apart from the occasional red-rimmed eye, nobody was showing any sign that two of their colleagues had recently died. Stable lads and lasses scurried about as several horses were being loaded on to a transporter along with all their tack. Directing the operation in a loud Irish accent was a tall woman in riding boots and jodhpurs. Her long curly hair was the colour of conkers.

"Siobhan, the police are here to see you. This is Chief Inspector Shadow and Sergeant Chang," said Clancy tentatively before politely stepping out of the way. Siobhan nodded in their general direction, but her eyes remained fixed on a large grey stallion that didn't seem too keen on the idea of going into the transporter. Shadow was about to offer Siobhan his hand, but noticing she was holding a bridle in one and a crop in the other cleared his throat instead.

"Good morning, Mrs FitzAllan. Thank you for seeing us and may I first offer our condolences on the loss of your husband and Mr O'Doyle. I understand this must be a difficult time for you, but would it be possible for you to answer a few questions?"

"Ask away, Chief Inspector, but I don't have much time with Flynn and now Aidan gone. I'm left to do the work of three people, and we need to be in York in less than two hours."

Shadow nodded. From her attitude there certainly didn't seem for any need to tiptoe around the new widow, so he got straight to the point.

"Can you tell us when you last saw your husband?"

"He swanned off yesterday morning to see his hoity-toity friends, leaving me to do all the graft, again, and on the eve of the Ebor meeting. ''Tis important to socialise with the owners,' he'd say. Socialising my arse! He was only there for the craic. As for Aidan! He swore to me he'd stay with Moon all night and what did he do? Drank himself into a stupor then went and got himself run over. Honestly, I'm surrounded by eejits!" she exclaimed as she pointed at a quivering groom. "Where is Native's saddle?" she screeched at the red-faced young man. "Do you expect his jockey to ride him bareback? You're not at the Tipperary Fair now. You great lummox!"

Thanks to studying the *Racing Post* in the car, Shadow understood that Moon and Native were Voodoo Moon and Native Friend, two horses that were due to run that day. He pressed on despite the ever-increasing chaos in the yard.

"I think I should inform you that it was one of our own officers whose car hit Mr Doyle. He was off duty at the time," explained Shadow. Siobhan finally glanced in his direction.

"I bet the poor sod's shaken up. Don't worry—you'll get no grief from me on that score. What did Aidan think was going to happen to him, sprawled out across the road like that?"

"When did you last see Mr O'Doyle?"

Siobhan shrugged.

"It would have been about seven. That's when I left York and I was back here about eight, maybe a bit after. When we'd unloaded, I went to bed. Isn't that right, Clancy?" she asked the younger woman, who immediately nodded her head in agreement. Shadow scanned the yard and quickly counted up the grooms who were dashing back and forth. There were six in total, the same number who had been huddled together in the pub last night.

"Are all your staff present here today?" he asked.

"Yes, this is the lot of them—neither use nor ornament half the time."

Shadow wasn't sure if that was fair, but it did mean they all had an alibi for the time of Aidan's death, just as those at the shoot could back each other up over Flynn's death. It was frustrating to say the least.

"Did you telephone your husband at all yesterday?"

"Why would I waste my time doing such a thing? What use would he be to me, all dressed up in his tweeds, pretending to be lord of the manor?"

"Can you think of anyone who may have wished your husband harm?" Shadow persisted, despite Siobhan continuing to be distracted by her four-legged charges. "Somebody he had argued with? We heard that there had been some disagreement with Lady Victoria DeVere."

"Plum!" snorted Siobhan. "She's a right old wagon. Always harping on about animal rights. She swans around like she's the Mother Teresa to all things four-legged. That's all very well for someone who's never had to work for a living. She's practically turned Bluebell Farm into a refuge, taking in every waif and stray going, and then encouraging sabs to come into the village."

"Sabs?" enquired Jimmy nervously, when Siobhan paused briefly to take a breath. He was rewarded with a contemptuous look.

"Saboteurs!" she almost spat out. "The place was swarming with them last year. Trying to disrupt the hunt or shooting parties. They turned up here with their placards a few months back. I soon told them where to go with their crusty hair in dreadlocks and stinking of hemp! Wastrels the lot of them!"

Shadow had to hand it to Siobhan, she could fling around an impressive array of insults.

"Getting back to Mr O'Doyle, was he aware of Mr FitzAllan's death? Was he upset by the news?"

"He was. I told him as soon as Clancy phoned me, but I told him clear as day, it wasn't the time to start blubbing. The best thing he could do for Flynn now was to take care of Legend and he couldn't even do that right."

"Would that be Kirkdale Legend?" asked Shadow becoming more grateful for Maggie's newspaper by the second.

"That's right, although he's more of a liability than a legend. He should be a champion. His mother won the Thousand Guineas, and his father won the St Leger. He can run like the wind out on the gallops but take him to a course and he goes on strike. I swear he thinks he's on holiday. We took him and Wantage Whisper yesterday. Whisper's a calming influence. I've got high hopes for him at York. I only pray this business with Aidan hasn't upset him too much."

Shadow couldn't help noticing Siobhan seemed far more concerned about the horses than her employees or her husband. The last horse due to be loaded on to the transporter suddenly reared up and Siobhan jumped forward to grab his lead rein and began barking more instructions. Shadow decided this was their cue to leave, so he thanked her and wished her luck, but she barely acknowledged him. Clancy escorted them back to their car.

"I know we asked you yesterday but are you positive nobody here contacted Mr FitzAllan? You see the screen of his phone was damaged when we found it. Could he have heard some bad news and smashed it out of anger or frustration?"

The young woman shook her head. "No, I asked around after you'd gone yesterday, but nobody called him and to be honest, Chief Inspector, Flynn wasn't the smashing things type. Siobhan used to say he was so laid-back he was horizontal." Clancy's face flushed a little. "I know what you must be thinking, but Siobhan and Flynn had...well their marriage was more like a working relationship than a romance. They led pretty separate lives."

"What about Mrs FitzAllan's relationship with Mr O'Doyle?"

"Aidan and Siobhan never really saw eye to eye," replied Clancy, sounding a little apologetic. Shadow privately wondered if Mrs FitzAllan ever saw eye to eye with anyone that didn't have a mane and a tail.

"Was Siobhan here alone last night or did someone stay with her?" he asked.

"She was on her own. I offered to stay, but she said she'd rather be alone. Some of the stable lads live on site in a flat above the horses in the yard, but I think everyone was in the pub until last orders," explained Clancy. "Oh, that reminds me, here's the list of everyone who works here. I thought you might find it useful, but I'm sorry I don't have any contact details for Aidan's next of kin. He never really talked about his family back home much," she apologised as she produced a sheet of paper from her folder and handed it over to Jimmy. They continued walking past the paddock where six or seven horses stood munching grass and swishing flies away with their tails.

"How come they get to spend the day grazing in the sun? Are they retired?" asked Jimmy.

"No not exactly, these are all horses that compete in National Hunt racing, you know over the jumps, so they only race in the winter months. Oh, and that handsome chestnut chap over in the corner is Parnell. He's the love of Siobhan's life. They used to compete together. They were quite the team."

"Siobhan was a jockey?" asked Shadow.

Clancy smiled and shook her head.

"No, she's too tall to go on the flat or even over the jumps, but she used to be a champion in endurance and cross-country back in Ireland. That's how she met Flynn. He was the vet to the Irish team. When she retired from competing, they decided to start training horses together."

"I see," said Shadow. "Could I ask you about another incident? You may not remember it, but about a week ago, Flynn had red wine spilt on a shirt and his suit jacket. We wondered if you knew what happened."

Clancy flushed a little, but she nodded her head. "Yes, I do remember. He looked a real mess when he got back. He'd been at Ripon during the day. Siobhan and the horses arrived back hours before him. He said he'd called in to Sir Charles Richmond's for dinner on the way home and that's when he spilt it. Why is that important?" asked Clancy, looking puzzled.

"Oh, it probably isn't, but we're trying to build up a picture of his life during the time leading up to his death," replied Shadow smoothly.

"I see, well, be sure to let me know if you need anything else. Take care now."

She waved goodbye as the two detectives climbed back into their car. Jimmy started the engine and began to negotiate a tight three-point turn. Shadow was deep in thought, replaying the conversations they'd just had.

"What did you make of Siobhan, Chief?" asked Jimmy then, before Shadow could reply: "She's pretty fiery, isn't she? You wouldn't want to cross her, would you? I bet she could have thrown a glass of wine over Flynn."

"I think she's more likely to have smashed the whole bottle over his head," grunted Shadow. When Maggie had first told him the story, he had assumed the wine throwing had been the work of a wronged wife. Now having met Mrs FitzAllan, he wasn't sure she cared enough about her husband to react strongly to him having an affair. There was something else Siobhan had said that was bothering him. He turned to his sergeant. "What did you think about the way she described Aidan? She said he was sprawled across the road—perhaps it's simply a figure of speech, but it sounded like a graphic description."

"You mean as though she had seen him?"

"Possibly. Check exactly what time she left the racecourse and when she arrived back here at the Grange—ideally with someone who doesn't work for her and isn't terrified of her."

"No need, Chief, I can confirm that," replied Jimmy. Shadow looked at him in surprise.

"Do you mind telling me how?"

"We passed her as we were leaving the castle. Don't you remember? I was about to pull out and had to brake when she came around the corner, but she still beeped her horn and gave me the finger."

"You sure it was her?"

"Positive."

"Were you in danger of crashing into her?"

"Nowhere near! I was still on the driveway, but I guess her temper doesn't improve when she's behind the wheel."

"Or she wanted to make sure we'd seen her and remembered her," mused Shadow.

Jimmy turned and frowned at him. "But our car's unmarked. How would she have known who we were?" he asked.

"It wouldn't be difficult around here, where everybody knows each other. Suppose Clancy called her to say the police had been to the yard, two male officers in a black Audi and the driver was wearing a leather jacket and sunglasses. Then on her way home, Siobhan saw us leaving the castle and now you are her alibi," Shadow explained and shook his head. "Talk about perfect timing. She couldn't have planned it much better if she'd tried."

They carefully pulled away from the Grange and waved to the two waiting uniformed officers as the swarming press clicked their cameras and shouted out questions. As they drove away, Jimmy interrupted Shadow's thoughts again.

"Clancy seems nice doesn't she, Chief?"

"Yes, she does," agreed Shadow, "but she doesn't have much of an alibi."

Jimmy looked perplexed. "But we saw her and Giles walking over to their cottage."

"Being at home with your boyfriend isn't as solid as being in a crowded pub all night or being spotted driving home by two police officers."

Despite having made an appointment this time, their welcome at the castle was no warmer. Jarvis showed them to the library once more. He informed them that the duke was regrettably indisposed, but Shadow would be able to interview Sir Charles and also Lord and Lady Eastwold who were all at the shoot and had stayed at the castle following last night's party.

"This feels like being in one of those country house murder mysteries, Chief," whispered Jimmy as he turned on his electronic notebook and settled into one of the armchairs after the butler had left them.

"That's probably because we are in a country house and investigating a murder that is currently a mystery," replied Shadow irritably. He had decided to remain standing by the empty fireplace. The sun was streaming into the room through the French windows, and he found he was dazzled wherever he tried to sit down.

Piers Eastwold was the first to be shown in. He was tall with blue eyes and blond hair that was beginning to thin. Shadow guessed he was about the same age as the duke and that as a young man he must have been handsome, but he now had the flushed cheeks and bloodshot eyes of a heavy drinker. Without bothering to return Shadow's greeting, he went straight to the silver tray on the table and poured himself a large whisky, then yanked the heavy velvet curtain across the glass door to block the offending sun.

"That's better. I've got the mother of all hangovers," he declared before flopping down on the sofa opposite Shadow.

"Could you describe the events leading up to Mr FitzAllan's death yesterday, please Lord Eastwold?" he asked politely.

"What is there to say? We had lunch, Flynn went to make a call and he didn't come back."

"Make or take a call?" asked Shadow.

"What's the difference?" asked Eastwold with a shrug as he took a sip of his drink.

"Well, did someone call him, and he left to answer it, or did he say he needed to phone someone?" persisted Shadow, but Eastwold just shrugged again.

"I can't remember. I really wasn't paying that much attention," he replied sounding bored.

"What do you think happened to him?" asked Shadow. Eastwold looked at him as though he thought he was quite dim.

"Well, he was shot wasn't he? Maybe his gun went off by mistake, maybe he had bad news over the phone and decided to top himself. How should I know? Isn't it your job to find out?"

"Indeed it is, and we don't believe his wounds were self-inflicted."

"Then maybe someone was lying in wait for him."

"Do you have anyone in mind?"

"I don't know—some psycho who should have been locked up or kids messing around." Eastwold yawned widely before taking a large slug of whisky.

"Do you have children yourself, Lord Eastwold?" asked Jimmy, looking up from his note taking.

"Yes, twin boys. Eight years old. It's been good to get away from them for some peace and quiet. Thank God the little buggers are going to prep school in September," he replied before throwing the last of his drink down his throat. Shadow didn't think they were going to find out anything more useful from His Lordship, so he thanked him for his time and decided to move on to another witness.

Lady Eastwold arrived next. Lavinia was about ten years older than her sister the duchess. She had long light brown hair, a large wide mouth and was wearing a long floaty, floral-print dress that she was both too short and too plump to carry off. She was certainly more loquacious but no more helpful than her husband.

"The shooting here at Kirkdale is always wonderful and Bertie is such a good host. I can't wait until my boys are old enough to join us. Bertie is also a very generous uncle," she gushed, arranging herself in the seat recently vacated by Lord Eastwold.

"Am I correct in thinking he doesn't have any children of his own?" asked Shadow.

"No. Thankfully there's at least one area where I've succeeded, and Annabel has failed. As Bertie said, 'Good girl, Lavinia, right first time. An heir and a spare!'" Lavinia giggled self-consciously. "Although, I suppose the fault probably does lie with him. Sybil is convinced the scarlet fever he had as a child damaged his heart and, well, other things, so no babies for Annabel. Poor thing."

As Lady Eastwold sat there with a smug smile, Shadow wondered if she knew her husband was less than enthusiastic about their offspring.

"Your children are eight years old, but your sister only married the duke about a year ago?" asked Jimmy looking up from his notes. "Does that mean you knew him before your sister met him?"

Lavinia laughed as if the sergeant had just told the most brilliant joke.

"Of course! I've known Bertie for yonks! He and Piers have been best friends forever. In fact, we were the ones who introduced Bertie and Annabel, not that she's ever thanked me. I have quite the gift when it comes to bringing people together."

Jimmy dutifully noted all this down and Shadow was about to ask another question when she began to twitter again.

"I don't know why you are wasting our time with this Flynn business. It must have been a horrible accident and if it wasn't, then we've already told you nobody saw a thing. If I were you, I'd go and speak to Plum, Bertie's sister. She was always arguing with Flynn. Personally, I think she's probably frustrated."

"She married a second cousin, I believe," said Shadow thinking back to what he'd read in *Debrett's* during the drive to Kirkdale.

"That's right Sir Peter DeVere, so at least she got to keep her name. They were teenage sweethearts and both equally insufferable. Trotting around Africa or South America on some do-gooding cause or other. Then he went and died not long after Seb was born."

"Oh, that's really sad," commented Jimmy.

"Not really, Sergeant," replied Lavinia briskly. "He was only a baronet. Plum could have done much better."

SIR CHARLES WAS the last to arrive for his interview. A widower of about sixty, he had represented his constituency for over twenty years after a successful career in the city. He was a member of the Home Office Select Committee and a vocal supporter of the police. A dapper dresser who wore his thick grey hair in an immaculate quiff, he was a favourite of the Westminster sketch writers. He shook hands with both of the detectives, before taking a seat when he was invited.

"Well, this is a nasty business, gentlemen. I liked Flynn very much. Such a waste of a life." He paused and looked up. "How can I help you?" he asked.

"Can you describe the events leading up to the discovery of Mr FitzAllan's body yesterday?" asked Shadow, hoping the MP's response to this enquiry would be more helpful than the Eastwolds'.

"Certainly," began Sir Charles, clearing his throat. "We all met here in the breakfast room at half past nine. The Eastwolds and I had spent the previous evening here. The three of us were here last night too. Flynn was the last to arrive, then we all headed up to the moor."

"So that was you, Mr FitzAllan, the duke and Lord and Lady Eastwold all in the same car?" asked Shadow.

"No, Lady Eastwold drove up alone a little later—I believe she had something she wanted to discuss with Annabel first—but the rest of us were in the duke's car. Bertie was driving."

"And how was everyone?"

Sir Charles shrugged.

"Fine, I think. We chatted about shooting and the racing of course."

"Mr FitzAllan didn't seem preoccupied or worried?"

"Not at all, he was his usual relaxed, easy-going self. He certainly did better than the rest of us put together on the first drive."

"Did you know Mr FitzAllan well? I understand you and the duke are both on the board of directors at York racecourse."

"That's correct. I wouldn't say Flynn and I were particularly close, but our paths have crossed fairly regularly over the last ten years or so."

"Is it true that he had dinner at your house a few weeks ago following a race meeting at Ripon?"

Sir Charles's brow furrowed, and he shook his head. "No, I'm sorry, Chief Inspector. I don't you know where you got that information from, but it's not true. I haven't entertained at home in any way, shape or form since I lost my wife five years ago. Naturally, I still like to socialise and repay the hospitality I have been lucky enough to receive, so a few times a year I host a dinner at my club in London, but I don't recall Flynn ever attending."

"Then we must have been mistaken," replied Shadow easily. "Going back to yesterday, you broke for lunch at about twelve thirty?"

"Yes, Lavinia—Lady Eastwold—had joined us by then. There was a table set up in the old chapel with a buffet: sandwiches, salads, that sort of thing. Then as we were leaving, Flynn said he needed to make a call. He walked over to the copse. He said the signal was better there."

"Did he say who he was calling?"

"No, I assumed it was the yard or Siobhan, but he didn't say."

"Do you know if he was responding to a missed call or a text message?" asked Shadow, silently cursing forensics. This line of questioning would be a lot easier if they had provided all the information from the burner phone.

"Again, he didn't say, but I did see him scrolling through his phone while we were at lunch, as was I, I might add. The signal up on the moor is terrible, so I missed quite a few calls."

"Did he look angry or upset at all?"

Sir Charles was silent for few seconds. "Now you come to mention it, I'd say he looked confused. That's how I'd describe his expression: puzzled or confused."

Shadow nodded thoughtfully. "I see and what happened after lunch?"

"We began the second drive without him. Then when he hadn't returned after about twenty minutes, Bertie spoke to his gamekeeper and he sent one of the loaders to look for him. We waited about five minutes, then the young man came running back and told us he'd found Flynn. As soon as we heard that we all dashed over and it was clear there was no point calling for medical assistance, so someone phoned you chaps."

"I understand the gun Mr FitzAllan was using, the Lumley, was quite special. A rare and valuable antique."

"Yes. Xander, Bertie's father, left it to Flynn in his will."

"Did anyone think that was unusual?" queried Shadow with a frown.

"No, not especially. Flynn wasn't only a gifted horseman, he was also an excellent shot and Xander had known him since his time in Ireland. In fact, I think he even paid for Flynn's tuition at university."

"Really?" asked Shadow. This was the first time he'd heard that Flynn was connected to the late duke in any way other than training his racehorses.

"So I understand, although I'm not sure if it was a general scholarship in the DeVere name or a more personal arrangement."

"Didn't the current duke mind his father leaving such a valuable gun to an outsider?" asked Jimmy, looking up again from his note taking. Shadow raised his eyes to the ceiling. Would he ever get through an entire interview without Jimmy interrupting?

"You will have to ask Bertie how he felt, Sergeant," replied Sir Charles, "but I can't imagine he would care too much. He inherited quite a collection of guns without the Lumley and then there's the pair of Purdeys his father bought him when he turned eighteen. Lucky sod! My father didn't even buy me a pint for my eighteenth."

"We'll have to talk to the duke another time, unfortunately," said Shadow before Jimmy could start asking another question. "We were told that he's indisposed this morning."

"Indisposed?" Sir Charles grinned again. "That's a new one on me!" Then registering the puzzled looks to the detectives' faces: "Bertie rather overdid it at the party last night. I expect he's busy knocking back aspirin and Alka-Seltzers before we head off to the races this afternoon. We are due to leave in a couple of hours."

"Then we won't keep you any longer," replied Shadow holding out his hand to the MP. "Thank you for your time, Sir Charles."

"Not at all. Good luck with the investigation, Chief Inspector."

He stood up and was almost at the door when Shadow remembered something.

"Oh, one more thing, Sir Charles. The police at the gates, who requested them?"

"I did, Chief Inspector, for Annabel's sake more than anything. The press are always hounding her even though she's given up modelling. You know what the tabloids are like. This business is bound to make it worse. She shouldn't be made to feel under threat in her own home. I asked for a couple of officers to go to Siobhan's too. I'm sure she doesn't need the extra hassle either."

"I see. Thank you again, Sir Charles," replied Shadow.

"Why did you ask him that?" asked Jimmy as soon as Sir Charles had left the library. "The chief constable told you it was him who asked for someone to keep the press out."

"I know, but I wanted to see what he would say," said Shadow as he opened the curtain Eastwold had closed. "I thought it was interesting the request came from him and not the duke."

Sir Charles was followed by the seven members of staff who worked permanently in the castle including Jarvis the butler. All told a similar story. The shooting party including

Mr FitzAllan had met in the morning room and then left for the shoot. Lady Eastwold had remained behind talking to the duchess for about half an hour before leaving too. The duchess was at home all day but spent several hours alone in her rooms. The whole party returned early after what all the staff referred to as the shooting incident.

When Shadow and Jimmy finally stepped out of the library, they saw Annabel walking down the long corridor towards them. Already dressed for the race meeting, she was wearing an elegant pale pink suit and matching hat. Shadow was sure it was very fashionable, but it did rather look like a flying saucer had landed on her head.

"Good morning," he said politely, but she didn't acknowledge him as she glided by. "I don't believe you told us where you were yesterday afternoon," Shadow continued.

Annabel paused, but only half turned her head. "I was here preparing for the party."

"Your staff mentioned you were alone and unseen for several hours?"

"The servants are here to serve not spy on me," she replied coolly before continuing on her way.

"Was Mr FitzAllan invited to the party?" Shadow called after her, but he received no response.

"Maybe she's hungover too," whispered Jimmy.

"Ha!" A voice behind them gave a sharp laugh, causing both detectives to spin round in surprise.

Lavinia was perched on a gilt chair in the hall, flicking

through one of the glossy magazines that were artistically arranged on a low leather stool. She gave them a tight smile.

"Annabel doesn't drink, gentlemen! Think of the calories!"

"Ah, Lady Eastwold, I understand you stayed behind to speak with the duchess, before joining the rest of the shooting party. May I ask what you discussed?" asked Shadow.

"It was just a girly chat between sisters, Chief Inspector," Lavinia replied with a simper.

WHEN THEY FINALLY stepped outside Jimmy exhaled loudly as they walked back to their car.

"Wow, Chief! The Eastwolds are both awful. How do the duke and duchess put up with them?"

"They are family. I suppose they have to," replied Shadow with a shrug.

"Sir Charles seemed okay," continued Jimmy as they climbed back into the car. "I was surprised he wants to hang around with the Eastwolds and the DeVeres."

"People like being associated with titles and don't forget Sir Charles is a politician. The duke, although arguably not the sharpest knife if the drawer, gets to sit in the House of Lords thanks to our hereditary upper chamber. While Sir Charles sits in the Commons, perhaps he finds an association with the duke useful."

"That sounds a bit mercenary. I don't think I'd last long in politics."

"No, Sergeant, neither do I."

"And the duchess. I don't get it. She's got everything. Beauty, money, a title—she even lives in a massive castle, but she seems really miserable. And I don't think her sister likes her much either."

"Then maybe psychology isn't your strong point either. Jealousy can be a dangerous emotion."

"How do you mean, Chief?"

"Never mind. The more pressing question is who's lying: Clancy, Flynn or Sir Charles?"

"Chief?"

"About the dinner, Sergeant, that according to Sir Charles didn't take place. Is he lying to us, did Clancy lie, or did Flynn lie to her?"

"I don't think it's Clancy. It must be Flynn. We already know he told Maggie a different story about how he spilt wine on himself. Do you really think it's important?"

"Maybe or maybe not. I just don't like loose ends."

They drove down the long driveway. Thankfully the press seemed to have disappeared, but the two constables were still waiting dutifully. Before they pulled through the huge wrought-iron gates, Shadow turned to Jimmy.

"Stop here and let me out, will you?"

"Why, Chief?"

"It's your lucky day, I want you to put on the siren and

do your best Lewis Hamilton impression. Let me know the shortest time possible to drive from here to the Lucky Horseshoe."

"Do you think someone staying at the castle killed O'Doyle?"

"I don't know, but at the moment the four who were shooting with FitzAllan were also here when O'Doyle died. The same people are giving an alibi to each other. If we are linking O'Doyle's and FitzAllan's deaths, then I want to know if any of them could have got to York in time to hit him. Could one of them have sneaked out and not have been missed for an hour or so? It sounds like a fair amount of alcohol was consumed, so memories might be hazy."

"Then surely we can discount the duke and Eastwold," interrupted Jimmy. "It sounds like they were both plastered."

Shadow shook his head. "No, we don't have any proof of that, only what we've been told. We didn't even get to speak to the duke. Now, admittedly, anyone leaving here wouldn't be in a police car, but the roads would be quiet that time of night. I want to know how quickly they could have got there and back. Then when you get to the Lucky Horseshoe, go and speak to the landlord. I know uniform took a statement last night, but make sure they didn't miss anything."

CHAPTER FIVE

Down 1. An infidelity when Fiona and Anthony are seen at the fair (6 letters)

S HADOW STEPPED OUT of the car and watched as his sergeant sped off with wheels spinning, gravel flying, and a huge grin on his face. Then he walked the few paces back to the door of the gatehouse with the lace curtains and knocked. He had a few seconds to notice the neatly planted vegetable garden before the door was opened by Bill, the elderly man with ruddy cheeks and a neatly trimmed beard who had greeted Shadow and Sybil yesterday near the greenhouses.

"Good morning. My name is Chief Inspector Shadow. May I come in?"

"Bill Greenwood," the man replied, shaking Shadow's outstretched hand, before moving to one side. "You look just like your dad, and your granddad for that matter."

Shadow stepped through the door into a small but cosy room that doubled as both a kitchen and a sitting room. There was a well-scrubbed pine table and an old-fashioned wood-burning range that acted as both stove and heater, making the place almost uncomfortably warm on such a hot day. In the corner there was a door that Shadow assumed led to the bedroom. Bill gestured to one of the faded striped sofas and Shadow sat down.

"If you can remember them both then you must have worked on the estate for a long time," he said.

"I was gamekeeper here for forty years, before my son took over. Now I help out in the castle gardens, more as a hobby than anything else," explained the older man as he went to open one of the small leaded light windows, which let in a welcome breeze. "I was here the night your dad was killed. Just in those woods over there." He pointed to the woodland that began a few yards from his house and separated the castle from the village.

"Was it you who saw the poachers and called him out?"

Bill shook his head. "No that was Edna my wife. She thought she saw a light in the woods. I was out checking some pheasant chicks on the other side of the estate and she couldn't find me. We didn't have mobile phones in those days of course, so instead of waiting, she phoned the police house. That was Edna though, always had to get involved. Your father came straight out, and well, you know the rest."

"Who found his body?" asked Shadow.

"I did. As soon as I arrived home, Edna told me what she'd done, and I went to the woods. I found him after about ten minutes, but it was too late. I came back here and called an ambulance and the police, but we didn't find anyone else." He was silent for a moment. "I've often sat here going over what happened that night."

Shadow's eyes scanned the room. It was tidy enough, but rather like *Florence*, it didn't look as though a woman lived there.

The old man seemed to read his mind. "Edna died five years ago."

"I'm sorry," said Shadow. Over the years he'd always pushed thoughts of his father's death to the back of his mind and his mother had never wanted to discuss it but speaking to the old gamekeeper and looking at the woods where he'd been found made it feel as though it had happened only recently. Then he remembered something that had been bothering him.

"Your son didn't refer to what happened that night, when he was speaking to us about Mr FitzAllan. He said nothing like it had ever happened before."

"No, well, it happened before he was born. After-wards—" the old man shifted in his seat; he looked embarrassed "—people didn't like to talk about it and then you and your mother moved away."

"Sybil recalled the incident as soon as she heard my name," said Shadow.

"Well, that's Her Grace for you," Bill said with a smile. "Ever since she arrived here in the village, even though she was only nineteen when she married the duke, she's always cared about the estate and the people who live here. It's important to her that everything is run right." He paused, and his smile faded. "I think she always felt guilty about what happened to your father."

"Why?"

"That night His Grace—that is, the late duke—was away in Ireland. She was here with Bertie; he was only a baby then. The castle was full of staff, but she felt the estate was her responsibility while her husband was away and your dad, well he died on her watch. Maybe that's another reason nobody liked to talk about it, for fear of upsetting her."

"And so my father was forgotten about?" asked Shadow, unable to keep the edge out of his voice.

"Not by everyone," Bill said firmly, then paused again. "I remember you coming to visit your grandparents when you were a lad. They were so proud of you. They were good people." He gave a slight smile. "And nobody could make apple pies like your grandma."

Shadow stood up to leave. He had a feeling the old man had told him everything he wanted to and now he really needed to focus on more recent events for George's sake if nothing else. He couldn't afford to be distracted by the events surrounding his father's death.

"Before I go, can I ask you where you were yesterday afternoon?"

"When the horse trainer was shot you mean? I was working up in the castle gardens, like I am most days. Before lunch I went to ask if the new duchess wanted any flowers in particular for the evening's party. There's always a big display of fresh blooms on the dining table when there's company. Jarvis told me Her Grace was locked in her bathroom preparing for the party and had asked not to be disturbed."

"So, there were no flowers for the party?" enquired Shadow.

The old man looked quite shocked by this suggestion and shook his head vehemently.

"Of course there were flowers. I saw the dowager duchess in the greenhouses after I'd spoken to Jarvis and told her what he'd said. Then later in the afternoon she picked the flowers she wanted and made up three beautiful arrangements herself. She's always been blessed with green fingers," he explained. Shadow noticed the tips of his ears turning pink as he talked about Sybil.

"What flowers did she use?" asked Shadow as he reached for the door handle.

"Roses with camellias and gardenias from the greenhouses. They've done well this year."

Shadow thanked him for his time and left the cottage, grateful to escape the oppressive heat and talk of the past.

IT TOOK ABOUT twenty minutes for him to stroll from the gatehouse into the village. On the way he walked along the babbling stream that fed into the duck pond. There were three wooden benches on the verge overlooking the pond. A young mother and a little girl were sitting on one, tearing up slices of stale bread to throw to the quacking ducks who were gathering at the edge of the water. Shadow paused for a moment and watched. He had a distant memory of doing the same thing with his mother. He wished he had more memories of his father. It had felt very odd after all these years to talk to someone who could remember him, better than he did himself.

As he wandered through the village, he approached St Michael's and took a detour through the churchyard. He stopped in front of the two headstones marking the graves of his father and grandparents. His grandma and grandad shared the same plot. Shadow didn't give his own death a great deal of thought, but now he wondered where he would end up. When Luisa had died, her parents had insisted on taking her body back to Italy. He had most definitely not been invited to her funeral. He was so lost in his thoughts that he jumped when he felt a light tap on his shoulder.

"I'm sorry, Chief Inspector, did I startle you?"

He looked around in surprise to see Sybil standing behind him. She was holding a basket full of white roses.

"A little. I'm afraid I was distracted," he admitted.

"Well, I'm hardly surprised. I hear there's been another death; one of the grooms from the stables. It seems rather a strange coincidence," she said, then noticed the graves in front of them, "or perhaps your thoughts were a little closer to home. Are all your relatives buried here?"

"My father and grandparents are, and when my mother died, she left instructions that she wanted to be cremated and have her ashes scattered on my father's grave," explained Shadow a little awkwardly. He never spoke about his family to anyone.

"And did you carry out her wishes?" asked Sybil.

Shadow was a little taken aback. "Of course," he replied. Although his mother had never discussed it with him, it had never occurred to him to do anything other than what she requested in her will.

Sybil sighed. "I want to be cremated too and have my ashes scattered at the top of Sutton Bank. I like the idea of floating wild and free, looking out over this beautiful countryside, but I expect I'll end up here with the rest of the DeVeres." She nodded towards the ornately carved iron gate on the other side of the churchyard that led to the DeVere private family plot. It seemed the dukes and duchesses were separated from the rest of the village even in death.

"I'm sure if your family knows what you want, they will follow your instructions," said Shadow, hoping he sounded reassuring. Sybil gave a cynical little laugh.

"Perhaps Chief Inspector, but I learnt long ago that marrying into a family like my husband's means giving up a little of yourself and your own needs. You soon learn that all that really matters is preserving the estate and doing what's best for the family."

"Do you still live up at the castle?" asked Shadow. Sybil shook her head.

"No, Chief Inspector, I firmly believe a house can't have two mistresses. I moved out when Bertie moved Annabel in. I live in the dower house now. It's much more manageable." She pointed across the road to what was still a very large house built in York stone. There were pillars at the front door and the twisted branches of a wisteria covered the whole of the front elevation, so it seemed to be suffocating beneath the fat purple blooms. "Of course I still pop up to the castle most days. I like to keep an eye on what's happening in the gardens and Annabel isn't interested in earthy pursuits. She's far too cosmopolitan. I did expect her to keep disappearing off to London, but she hasn't left Kirkdale for months so we must hold some attraction for her. Perhaps it means she's discovered the appeal of village life."

"And perhaps the possibility of more grandchildren?" suggested Shadow tentatively.

Sybil arched an eyebrow and pursed her lips. "It sounds like Lavinia has been gossiping again." Then she sighed and shrugged her shoulders. "Not that it's much of a secret. Sadly, my son has suffered from poor health for years. A particularly nasty bout of scarlet fever when he was a child. Xander brought it back with him from Ireland and passed it on to the rest of us, except Plum of course. I swear she has the constitution of an ox. Poor Bertie suffered terribly though. It turned into rheumatic fever that weakened his heart. It even made him deaf for a while. The doctors said it wouldn't affect his fertility, but I'm not convinced." She paused and gave a small shrug. "But then all couples have their problems. Naturally, I would love another grandchild, but I'm lucky. Thanks to Plum I have my wonderful Seb, so our future is secure. Now if you will excuse me, Chief Inspector, I was just on my way to visit my husband's grave." She picked out four of the long-stemmed roses and handed them to Shadow. "Why don't you take these?"

"Thank you," replied Shadow. He watched her go through the gate then quietly laid two of the roses on each of the graves.

He left the church and walked a little farther. It was almost lunchtime, and the pub was already open. As he got closer, he noticed there were several cars parked outside. According to their number plates, they were all from London. So, this is where the press had ended up. Rather than enter the pub, he peered through the window. Several young men in sharp suits were standing at the bar listening to Bet hold court. She seemed to be enjoying herself and the tabloid journalists obviously thought local gossip was going to be a good source for their stories.

"If you want to avoid the hacks, there's a beer garden at the back, Chief Inspector," said a voice behind him. Shadow turned to see Giles standing next to him. The young man grinned. "I'm sure Bet will come and find you to take your order."

"Have they been here long?" asked Shadow nodding towards the journalists.

"A while, flashing the cash for a story about Flynn. They offered Fred a hundred quid to tell them who else was at the shoot, but they are wasting their time. I doubt anyone in the village will talk."

"Are you not working today?"

The young man was holding a large tub of salt in one hand and a bottle of white wine in the other.

"Not exactly, Chief Inspector. We rent our cottage from the estate and we have a yearly inspection. According to Clancy the next one is due soon and she's given me strict instructions to try and shift some red wine stains on the carpet in the living room. I went to ask Bet her advice. She said to pour white wine on first, then cover it in salt and hoover the lot up."

"Does that work?" asked Shadow genuinely interested. *Florence* had suffered more than her fair share of spilt red wine over the years and his solution was usually to strategically move the furniture around.

"No idea, but I'll let you know," said Giles with a smile, "and if it doesn't at least I can have a glass of sauvignon while I find out." He turned and headed back to his cottage with a wave. Shadow walked through the wooden gate Giles had pointed to and followed a cobbled path to a pretty garden dotted with picnic-style tables. Shadow sat at one that was shaded by an old apple tree and had a view across the valley towards the White Horse of Kilburn. The old chalk carving on Sutton Bank was dazzling in the bright sunshine. There was a gliding club up there and every few minutes a small plane flew off the edge towing a glider, before releasing it so the silent white craft could dive and swoop, carried on the rising thermals. He leaned back against the tree and thought about what Sybil had said about wanting her ashes scattered up there. Now he thought about it, he doubted there was a better place to end up.

"There you are! I thought I saw you sneaking past the window. You can't stay away, can you? What'll it be a pint and a ploughman's?" Bet had appeared in front of him. The leopard-print top had been changed for a zebra print, but it was equally low-cut and clinging.

"Er yes please," he said and then recalled something. "Did I see an ordnance survey map for sale on the bar yesterday?"

"Nothing gets past you, does it? That's right, we keep a small stock for any ramblers."

"Could I trouble you for one of those as well?"

"No trouble at all, my love."

She returned a few minutes later with his pint and the map.

Shadow unfolded the map and spread it out across the wooden table. He rummaged through his pockets until he found his glasses and a pen. He marked Kirkdale with an X and then located York racecourse and marked that too. He really needed a ruler or tape measure, but he didn't feel like asking Bet for another favour. Instead, he picked up one of the coasters and holding it against the scale rule on the map, made a mark equal to three miles along the edge of the coaster. Then using his improvised ruler he measured the distance in a straight line between the two X's. It was about twelve or thirteen miles.

Shadow leaned back in his chair and took a sip of his beer. Bees buzzed around the pink roses that were growing up the trellis and a tabby cat jumped up on the chair opposite him, stretched out and promptly fell asleep in the sun. He wanted to concentrate on Flynn and Aidan, but his mind kept drifting back to his father. He looked back at the map. The woods where his father died lay between the village and the castle. At that time of year, they would have been full of pheasants, no doubt very tempting for poachers.

His thoughts were disturbed by voices behind him. Men's voices. Slowly he peered around the edge of the tree, so he could see who was talking, but they couldn't see him. There were two men. One he didn't recognise, but the other was Lord Eastwold. Shadow strained his ears, but he couldn't make out what he was saying. He saw the other man hand a brown envelope over to Eastwold, then disappear back into the pub. Eastwold slipped the envelope into the inside pocket of his jacket, and a second later the duke stepped out of the pub kitchen door. He slapped his friend on the back and the two of them laughed at something. Then they walked towards the gate that led to the front of the pub.

He considered following them, but at that moment, Bet arrived with his lunch.

"There you go, Handsome! Enjoy! I'll keep popping back to check on you. I take it you are avoiding the gentlemen from the press."

"Are they still inside?"

"Oh yes. They seem to believe in a liquid lunch. And to think I thought my profits would be down without Flynn and poor old Aidan. I have to say it was quite a shock to hear we'd lost him too." She leaned forward and whispered, "Do you reckon someone is targeting the stables?"

"It's too early to say, I'm afraid," he replied not wanting to get involved with a discussion about the case. "Did the two of them drink here often?"

"Aidan was in every night; Flynn maybe once or twice a week."

"Were they close?"

Bet's face broke into a large smile.

"Aidan and Flynn? As thick as thieves. More like brothers than employee and employer. They'd grown up in the same village back in Ireland. After a few drinks they'd start telling stories about the old country. I always knew it was time for them to go home when they started singing 'Danny Boy' and 'Galway Bay'. Not that either of them could carry a tune." She laughed at the memory then stopped and her face fell. "It's not going to be the same around here without them."

Shadow nodded sympathetically. "Were either of them ever violent when they'd had a drink?" he asked, wondering if it was likely Aidan had got into a fight at the Lucky Horseshoe.

Bet shook her head so firmly that her long dangly gold earrings tinkled. "No never. I don't think Flynn had a violent bone in his body and Aidan was always very well behaved no matter how much he'd had." She lowered her voice. "He once told me he'd been in trouble with the law back in Ireland, so he wanted to keep his nose clean over here."

"Did he tell you what he'd done?" asked Shadow.

"He was involved in smuggling cigarettes across the border and one night he witnessed something he shouldn't, an assassination I think, and back then the only good witness was a dead one, so Flynn pulled a few strings and got him a job over here. When the old duke got Flynn over at the Grange to train his horses, Aidan joined him, and I don't think he ever went back."

"What about Mrs FitzAllan? Does she often come in here?"

Bet rolled her eyes dramatically. "Siobhan! No, thank God. She's got a nasty tongue in her head that one. We did a seafood festival last summer—you know putting dressed crab and mussels as specials on the menu. I set up a little cart outside to catch any passing trade. After that Siobhan started calling me Molly Malone. Cheeky cow! I don't know how Flynn put up with her."

Shadow murmured his agreement. "Did I just see Lord Eastwold and the duke here?" he asked.

"That's right, they popped in for a hair of the dog. Seems they're recovering from a heavy night. I wouldn't be surprised if those wives of theirs put them on rations today. Neither of them looks like they are much fun, do they?" Bet chuckled before she turned to go.

"By the way," said Shadow, "there's a broken dotted line on the map between the pub and church. According to the key, it's a disused path. Do you know anything about it?"

Bet leant forward revealing an ample amount of cleavage and peered at where Shadow was pointing.

"Oh, that must the old tunnel. It comes out in the cellar, but most of it has caved in. It was built when Catholic priests needed to escape, you know back when Henry the Eighth closed all the monasteries around here."

Shadow nodded. York was riddled with similar tunnels, but he'd never noticed them marked on a map before.

"Thank you that's very helpful," he replied edging away further along the bench.

"Don't mention it, Handsome! I told you I like coppers. I hope you're going to be sticking around. You're much more interesting than farmers talking about harvesting all day."

Shadow returned her flirtatious wink with a weak smile

and waited until she'd disappeared before turning his attention to the ploughman's lunch in front of him. He'd only taken a couple of bites of his pork pie when Jimmy arrived carrying a mineral water. Not wanting to disturb the slumbering cat he brought a chair over from one of the other tables.

"How long?" asked Shadow by way of a welcome.

"Thirty minutes there. I got held up in race traffic even with the siren on, but on the way back my foot was down flat all the way, and I did it in twenty-three minutes exactly, Chief."

"So, if you added ten minutes for dealing with Aidan, that would mean whoever it was would be away for an hour." He spread a thick layer of butter on a bread roll as he considered this new information for a moment, then shook his head. "I can't see it. Surely they would have been missed," said Shadow half to himself.

"Maybe they had someone covering for them. You know if anybody asked where's so and so, they'd say: oh he's just popped to the loo or stepped outside for a moment."

"Yes, thank you I understand the concept of covering for someone, Sergeant. Did you find anything out at the Lucky Horseshoe?"

"I showed the landlord a photo of Aidan. He remembered him even though the place was packed with other stable lads and grooms. He said Aidan sat alone all night. The news about Flynn had shocked everyone. Quite a few people went over to offer their condolences, but he didn't want to talk about it. To quote the landlord, 'If anyone was drowning their sorrows it was him.'"

"It sounds like he was more upset by Flynn's death than anyone. Bet told me the two of them were close."

"He left at about ten thirty. Everyone else stayed until closing time and by that time Aidan was dead."

"So, the place was packed, but nobody saw anything?"

"It doesn't sound like it. Sorry, Chief. Uniform have put up some notices asking for information around the stable area of the racecourse and when I left, they were doing another sweep of the area. They are still trying to find the weapon used to hit Aidan. Oh, that reminds me," said Jimmy suddenly taking his mobile out of his pocket, "Tom left a message while I was driving. He spoke to the Garda. Aidan's brother is in Cork, but he hasn't seen him for over twenty years. Apparently, he left Ireland in a hurry back in the nineties and hasn't been back since."

"That fits with what I've just heard too," replied Shadow, before briefly repeating the information from Bet for the benefit of his sergeant's notes.

"I suppose it's too much to hope that forensics have been back in touch?" asked Shadow, as Jimmy closed his electronic notebook.

"No sorry, Chief, I tried calling them both but neither of them were answering."

Shadow shook his head and grunted while Jimmy took a

sip of his water and nodded at the map.

"What's that for?"

"I was measuring the distance from Kirkdale to York. On the roads it's about twenty miles?" Jimmy nodded. "But as the crow flies it's about twelve or thirteen."

"To go over the fields you mean? That would take forever."

"Not if you were on a horse, a horse that's used to competing in endurance or cross-country."

Jimmy frowned until he realised what Shadow was implying. "Like Siobhan on Parnell?"

"Possibly. She doesn't have much of an alibi, and it sounds like she and Aidan didn't get on. Use that phone of yours and find out how fast an endurance horse could go cross-country?"

Jimmy removed his phone from his pocket and began clicking away. A few seconds later he looked up.

"Six or seven miles an hour, so she could have got back to York in a couple of hours. Time wise it would fit in, but would she be able to find her way? It would be getting dark by then."

Shadow wouldn't put anything past Mrs FitzAllan, but for now all he said was, "Well, it's something to think about. Let's make a move before our hostess comes back."

"Where to next, Chief?"

"I've asked Greenwood the gamekeeper to meet us up on the moor later this afternoon, but first let's pay the duke's sister a visit. Lady Eastwold, Bet and Siobhan all made a point of mentioning her to us."

ON THE WAY, Shadow flicked through his copy of *Debrett's*. He wanted to have the DeVere family dynamics clear in his head before another interview with a member of the clan. Lady Victoria DeVere lived on Bluebell Farm, about half a mile out of the village. It was a long, low white building with one of the few thatched roofs in the area. There was a courtyard with barns and stables and neatly fenced paddocks with an assortment of animals including donkeys, goats, sheep, chickens and even a couple of llamas strolling around in the sun. Bird feeders and nesting boxes were attached to almost every tree and much to Jimmy's delight, a squirrel scampered along the top of one of the fences.

When they stepped out of the car, a woman appeared from one of the stables. She was wearing cut-off denim jeans, flip-flops, and an old, checked shirt. Her long light brown hair was held back from her make-up-free face by a pink plastic hair clip. Her right hand was heavily bandaged. Shadow guessed she was in her early forties.

"Lady Victoria DeVere?" he asked, a little uncertainly. She looked a world away from Annabel and Lavinia, but the woman smiled and nodded, so he continued, "I'm Chief Inspector Shadow and this is Sergeant Chang," but before he could explain why they were there, Lady Victoria waved her good hand at him.

"Oh, just call me Plum; everybody does. Sorry I can't shake hands. I was late feeding Monty the other day and he took exception and decided to chomp on me instead." She waved towards a grumpy-looking billy goat glaring at them from the paddock. "I thought I'd be seeing you. Is it about poor old Flynn? Terrible business. I rather liked him, and he was very sexy. Gosh those eyes, that smile, and the accent alone was enough to make you go weak at the knees. He certainly shook the village up when he arrived. Of course, he and I didn't see eye to eye on everything, what with his line of business, but still, I'll miss him. And now I hear one of his grooms is dead too! Look, I'm sure you have lots to ask me, but it's terribly hot out here in the sun. Let's go to the Badger. We can have a sit-down and I can get you a cool drink."

Without waiting for a reply, she strode off across the courtyard. Shadow turned to Jimmy with a shrug and the two detectives obediently followed her. The Badger turned out to be the Tipsy Badger, a pub Plum had created in one of the old barns, complete with a hand-painted pub sign of a badger wearing a tiara and holding a glass of champagne. Inside beneath the exposed rafters was a fully functioning bar, with beer pumps, optics for the spirits and a fridge crammed full of champagne. Old oak wine barrels acted as tables, with stools set round them. There was even an old-fashioned jukebox in one corner.

"Welcome to the Tipsy Badger, my party room. Now what can I get you gentlemen?" asked Plum from behind the bar.

"Wow this place is great," enthused Jimmy. "An orange juice for me please."

"I'll have the same," agreed Shadow. He didn't entirely trust that his hostess was capable of pulling a decent pint. Plum plonked two glasses on the bar in front of them and fixed herself a gin and tonic.

"So, are you going to tell me all the juicy details?" she asked with a grin. "I saw Annabel earlier, but as usual she was keeping schtum. I often think my sister-in-law would have made an excellent spy. There was a rumour going around that Flynn had killed himself, well I don't believe a word of it. Flynn wasn't the type. What's the truth? Were Bertie and Piers boozed up? Did they get a bit trigger-happy? Will you be carting them off to jail?"

"Mum," said a voice from the corner of the room. "I think it's the police who are meant to ask you the questions, not the other way around."

Shadow and Jimmy turned around to see a young man working on a laptop at one of the tables.

"Seb, I didn't know you were in here. Was I gabbing too much again? Chief Inspector Shadow, Sergeant Chang, this is my son Sebastian," said Plum.

The tall young man stood up and politely shook hands

with the two detectives. Thanks to *Debrett's*, Shadow knew Seb's full name was Sebastian Peter Alexander DeVere. Shadow could understand why he shortened it to three letters. With his floppy blond hair, faded jeans and polo shirt, there was little to differentiate him from Giles and Fred, until he spoke. His voice was an upper-class drawl, without a trace of a Yorkshire accent. He joined Shadow and Jimmy sitting at the bar.

"I understand you are an animal rights supporter and that you disagreed, often publicly, with the way Flynn treated his horses," began Shadow, now Plum had finally shut up.

"Oh, not only Flynn, I disagree with horse racing in principle. I don't know how Flynn could call himself a vet and support it. Making those beautiful creatures run so fast, often in hot weather, then allowing jockeys to whip them to make them go faster. It's barbaric!" She shuddered dramatically.

"I take it you don't approve of your brother running a shoot either?"

"Certainly not! They have the nerve to call it sport. The day the pheasant and grouse have guns and can shoot back at them is the day it will truly be a sport. Things will be different when Seb takes over, won't they, darling?"

Plum reached over and ruffled her son's hair, who in return looked suitably embarrassed.

"Mum I won't inherit for years, maybe never."

"But you are the duke's heir?" asked Shadow. The family tree had been quite clear: if Bertie died childless, then his sister's son would become the next duke.

"Yes," Plum replied quickly before her son had a chance. "Bertie and Annabel don't have any children of their own and I can't see that changing anytime soon."

"How did the two of them meet?" asked Jimmy, earning himself a scowl from Shadow, who was more interested in pursuing Plum's certainty that they would not reproduce than the history of their relationship.

"Lavinia, Annabel's sister, introduced them. Lavinia is quite a bit older than Annabel. They are actually half-sisters. Their father Lord Wantage left Lavinia's mother for Annabel's. Mummy tells me it caused quite a stir at the time. The late Lord Wantage was a terrible gambler. He blew all his money and died when Annabel was just a teenager. She's been modelling and supporting herself ever since." Plum paused and took a sip of her drink. "Anyway, Lavinia married Piers about ten years ago, around the time her father died. Piers and Bertie have been best friends for years. When they were younger, they were always getting into trouble— drinking, gambling, driving too fast, encouraging each other. It used to drive Mummy and Daddy to distraction. It was Piers and Lavinia who introduced Annabel to Bertie when he was down in London. He was meant to be looking after Mummy. She'd had a stroke and was recovering in a hospital down there. Bertie shirked his responsibilities as usual." She shook her head as she took another sip. "Anyway, he must have thought it was about time he settled down and Annabel was growing bored of constantly having a camera shoved in her face, so that was that. I have to say we were all quite shocked. We had counted on Bertie remaining a bachelor forever."

Shadow thought he'd heard more romantic stories and Plum may have rambled on, but she had at least confirmed what Lavinia had told them. Before Jimmy could ask any more questions, Shadow turned his attention to Seb.

"Assuming you do inherit, don't you intend to keep the shoot going?" he asked.

The young man shook his head. "No, Grandpa made me go once when I was sixteen. I hated it. I won't allow fishing or any form of hunting either. The estate will still need income though of course, and I still plan to invite people up here to shoot—only with a camera, not a gun. I'd like to introduce species that were once popular in the area, but thanks to man's behaviour have disappeared. Otters in the river, maybe even beavers. They could help with some of the estate villages that are prone to flooding."

"That sounds great," enthused Jimmy.

Shadow glared at him. If he dared produce that damn wildlife book, he'd kill him.

Seb grinned. "Up in Scotland they are even introducing elk and wolves, but I'm not sure how our sheep farmers would feel about that."

"He's got so many wonderful ideas for the place, Chief Inspector," gushed Plum, beaming at her son. "Mummy agrees with me: he's going to make a fabulous job of running the estate and of course there won't be all Bertie's expenses like training fees for the horses. They can all come here and enjoy a lovely long retirement."

Shadow raised an eyebrow. He wondered what Siobhan would have to say about this idea.

"But like I said, it's years away," added Seb. "Granny said Uncle Bertie would have another coronary if I suggested he stop shooting. He still hasn't got over the hunting ban."

"Would you say you and your brother are close?" asked Shadow. He was addressing Plum, but Seb stepped in.

"I'm sorry, Chief Inspector, I don't mean to be rude, but is that relevant to how or why Mr FitzAllan died?"

Plum flapped her hand at him.

"It's fine, Seb, I don't mind answering. Bertie's a bully, Chief Inspector. He always has been. He made my life hell when we were children. Perhaps he was jealous when I came along and dared take some of our parents' attention away from him. It didn't help that I was brighter than him. Mummy used to excuse his appalling exam results by saying how ill he'd been as a child, but he really was a complete duffer. I'm afraid he was overindulged—the typical spoilt brat."

"Was he ever violent towards you?"

"No, it was more like emotional abuse. He'd pull the

heads off my favourite teddys and shut me up in one of the priest holes—that sort of thing. Then one summer when I was about ten years old, Peter was staying with us. He heard Bertie threaten to throw my kitten out of the window, egged on by Piers as usual. Peter punched Bertie so hard he broke his nose. From that moment, Bertie never bothered me again and I fell madly in love with Peter. He was my late husband and Seb's father, in case you didn't know, Chief Inspector. Naturally Mummy and Daddy were thrilled I would keep the name DeVere, so a happy ending all round."

Shadow nodded. Plum and Peter's story was certainly an improvement on Bertie and Annabel's.

"What are priest holes?" asked Jimmy, looking up from his electronic notebook.

"Back in the days when the country was swinging between being Catholic or Protestant, depending on who was on the throne, our ancestors liked to hedge their bets," Plum explained. "Outwardly they would be whichever religion was in vogue as it were, while still letting Catholic priests celebrate mass at the castle in case Protestantism was a passing fad. Of course, then they needed somewhere to hide the priests should the authorities come knocking."

"Like the tunnel between the pub and the church?" asked Shadow.

"Yes, that's right, Chief Inspector. There are holes and tunnels all over the castle and the estate," explained Seb. "Some are in better condition than others, so we have started some restoration work. I always thought it would be a good idea to open up the estate to the public and turn some of them into an attraction for tourists."

"You see I told you he's full of brilliant ideas," Plum enthused again.

"Siobhan FitzAllan mentioned something about you being associated with saboteurs," said Shadow.

"I bet she did," snorted Plum. "The woman's a dictator. I pity anyone who has to work for the witch."

Shadow raised an eyebrow. Clearly there was no solidarity amongst widows.

"I organised a perfectly legitimate protest outside the stables," she continued. "We didn't cause any damage and didn't trespass on to private land. It's true that some of those who attended might have, in the past, been involved with action against the local hunt if they suspected foxes were still being chased, but everyone there behaved responsibly. We were exercising our right to peaceful protest."

Shadow was a little surprised. Plum might seem dizzy, but when it came to legal matters, she sounded well informed.

"I understand Mr FitzAllan and your late father were close."

"Oh yes," agreed Plum, "Daddy adored Flynn. They had lots in common and of course it helped that since Flynn took over training Daddy's horses, he'd never had so many winners."

"And they knew each other before Flynn moved to Kirkdale?"

"Yes, Daddy invited him to set up at the Grange. Daddy was in the army when he was younger. He was posted to Northern Ireland during the Troubles and Flynn grew up in one of the border towns. I think that's when they met."

"When did he leave the army?" asked Shadow. This new information seemed to tie in with what Sir Charles had told them about the late duke paying for Flynn's education.

"Oh, ages ago and under a cloud I'm afraid." She paused. "I loved Daddy dearly, but I don't think soldiering came naturally to him. He only joined because his father wanted him to. Said Sandhurst would be the making of him."

Jimmy noted all this information down, while Shadow merely nodded, before asking, "Can you tell me where you both were yesterday afternoon, at around one o'clock?"

"I was here, Chief Inspector, painting. It's a great hobby of mine," Plum said gesturing to several watercolours of farm animals hanging on the wall.

"Was anyone here with you to confirm that?"

"No, sorry, but I can show what I was painting if you like?" she offered and before Shadow could reply she ducked behind the bar and carefully lifted a cardboard box up. She set it down gently and lifted the flap. Nestled inside among some hay was a hedgehog sleeping soundly. "We found him a few days ago. He'd fallen down one of the drains. The vet said he was underweight and dehydrated, so I'm feeding him up before releasing him into the wild," she explained. While Jimmy cooed over the snoozing hedgehog, Shadow turned to Seb.

"I take it that means you weren't here?"

"No, Chief Inspector, I was up on the moors taking some photographs."

"Did you see anyone?"

"No not until I was almost back in the village. Then I saw Granny walking back to the castle, so I gave her a lift. A couple of police cars went by. We both commented on it, but of course we didn't know then what had happened."

CHAPTER SIX

Down 6. Beatrice uses Brie to get what she wants (5 letters)

THE TWO DETECTIVES left Seb, Plum and the hedgehog behind and headed back to the moor. They turned on to the track that led up to the wooded area where the body had been found. In the distance, they could see Greenwood was waiting for them. Jimmy glanced at his phone as they left behind the copse and made their way across the moor towards the gamekeeper.

"The signal up here is rubbish," he complained. "I can't get any of my messages."

"At least we won't be interrupted," replied Shadow as they approached the gamekeeper. He held out his hand. "Thank you for agreeing to meet us again, Mr Greenwood."

"Not at all, Chief Inspector. What can I help you with?"

"We have established that Mr FitzAllan's wounds were not self-inflicted, so now we need to investigate the possibility that they were caused accidentally."

"A stray shot you mean?" The gamekeeper shook his head firmly. "No I can't see how that would be possible, Chief Inspector." He gestured behind him to the well-spaced little bunkers edged in stones. "These are the butts where each gun stands. You see we place sticks at the sides of each butt, so they know their boundaries. This way they don't get carried away and encroach on their neighbour's birds. Plus, all the guns, except Mr FitzAllan's, had a loader standing with them. To shoot towards the copse they would need to turn a full one-eighty. I'm sorry, Chief Inspector. I really don't see how that could have happened."

Shadow nodded as he walked between the butts. He understood what the gamekeeper meant. It would be almost impossible for a stray shot to have hit FitzAllan and even if one had, it didn't explain his head wound at close range.

"And you didn't see anyone on the track up to moor or near the old chapel? A walker or rambler maybe."

"No, Chief Inspector, this is private property. There aren't any public footpaths or bridle ways over the moor and besides, you wouldn't need to rely on any of us spotting a trespasser, there must have been about a dozen dogs up here. One of them would have sniffed out a stranger in seconds."

"Mr Greenwood," Jimmy began, and Shadow sighed to himself. He knew this tone. Jimmy was about to ask a question that no doubt would delay and divert the investigation. "What's the big deal with grouse?" Jimmy continued. "I mean the duke was throwing a party last night to celebrate the start of the season. What's so special about them?"

The gamekeeper frowned and was silent for a moment as he considered the question. "Well, they're small and faster than other birds, less predictable too, so they are harder to hit. You need more skill."

"Is that it?" asked Jimmy sounding disappointed. "They aren't worth a lot of money or anything?"

"It depends on how you look at it, Sergeant. I mean they might not be worth much if you were to buy them for eating, although my wife does a lovely roast grouse, but going on a commercial grouse shoot could cost you a few thousand pounds, not that His Grace charges anyone here. Anyone on his personal shoots is invited as a guest, but he does run a couple of commercial shoots on the moors above Helmsley."

Shadow decided it was time to interrupt before Jimmy moved on to enquiring about the merits of other game birds.

"Giles and Fred suggested that Mr FitzAllan was a particularly good shot. Is that true in your opinion?"

"I would say so yes, Chief Inspector. He was a natural." The gamekeeper paused and looked a little embarrassed. "And if I'm not speaking out of turn, he wasn't born to it not like the others. His Grace and Lord Eastwold have grown up shooting grouse, but as I understand it Mr FitzAllan had a very different upbringing back in Ireland. Not privileged, I mean."

"Yet the gun he used, the Lumley, was quite special I understand," said Shadow, hoping Greenwood would confirm what Sir Charles had already told them.

"It certainly is. It's a real beauty of a gun. It was a gift from His Grace—the late duke. He bequeathed it to Mr FitzAllan in his will."

"What about the pellets in the cartridges? Are they still made of lead?" asked Shadow recalling the information Ben and Ollie had sent, but not wanting to reveal too much to Greenwood.

"No, that is to say some are, but not here on the estate. Only cartridges with steel pellets are used."

"Why? Is it because of the risk of lead poisoning if you eat a bird shot with the old pellets?" asked Jimmy.

"Partly, Sergeant, but I'm sure I've swallowed plenty in my time and it hasn't done me any harm." The gamekeeper chuckled. "No to be quite honest, it was down to Lady Victoria. She gave her brother a bit of a lecture on wild birds getting poisoned when they mistake bits of spent pellets for grit or food. There was a talk of arranging a protest. The dowager duchess stepped in too and I think His Grace agreed to ban lead shot just to keep the peace."

Shadow thanked the gamekeeper for his time and privately wondered if he was aware of Plum and Seb's other plans for the estate and what that might mean for his livelihood and for his son's future.

"WHAT ARE YOU thinking, Chief?" asked Jimmy as they watched the gamekeeper stride back across the moor towards his Land Rover.

"That there might be something in one of your theories," replied Shadow.

"Really?"

"I know I'm surprised as you are, but what if what you said yesterday about one of the other members of the shooting party hitting FitzAllan by mistake was right? Could they have realised what they had done and shot him again with his own gun, in the hope of covering up what had really happened?"

"Greenwood just said it was impossible for FitzAllan to have been hit accidentally."

"He could be lying."

"Surely there would have been too many witnesses?"

"Probably but what if the witnesses owe their homes and livelihoods to the estate? Would they risk going against the duke's orders?" Shadow continued, thinking out loud.

Jimmy frowned next to him. "Like a conspiracy you mean, Chief?"

Shadow paused, shielding his eyes from the sun as he looked from the butts to the copse and back again.

"Oh, I don't know—perhaps it is a little far-fetched. I must have been spending too much time with you. Look, from here we can see the top of the trees in the copse and the roof of the ruined chapel. You go down to where we found the body. Let me see if FitzAllan would have been visible from up here on the moor."

Obediently Jimmy jogged away towards the trees. Shadow waited. After a few moments, his sergeant was out of sight. Satisfied that nobody on the moor could have seen FitzAllan, he trudged after Jimmy. The sun was beating down on his back. It really was far too hot to be roaming around like this. He'd walked about two hundred yards before the top of Jimmy's head came into view. When after a few more paces he arrived in the copse, Jimmy was wandering around holding his phone aloft.

"Could you see me, Chief?" he asked.

"No not until I was almost here," replied Shadow, who was now slightly out of breath.

"Well, that proves the rest of the party couldn't see him from up on the moor," Jimmy said. "And that this is one of the few areas up here with a decent mobile signal. My phone started bleeping as soon as I arrived here, but I only moved a few feet away and I lost it. So, what now, Chief?"

Shadow looked around them. There was a track leading back to the road; surely it would have been too risky to try and drive up here unseen. A little way along the track was the ruined chapel where the shooting party had eaten lunch. Shadow nodded towards it.

"Let's have a look in there and see if it's possible for someone to have hidden themselves and waited until Flynn was alone."

The ancient stone chapel was half covered in ivy. It had crumbled away in one corner and the tower and much of the roof had caved in thanks to the valuable lead having been stolen over the years since the reformation. However, when the two detectives stepped through the open doorway, and saw the beautifully carved stone pews and altar, it was quite easy to imagine the local farming families who must have once worshipped here hundreds of years ago. Shadow made his way towards the altar, assuming that was where the food and drink would have been laid out for the shooting party. He noticed a few remnants from the lunch. There was a picnic blanket folded on one of the pews and a corkscrew had been left behind.

"Can you get a picture of this? It might be worth asking forensics to take a look at it, although I don't why they didn't come in here yesterday."

"To be fair, we didn't ask them to, Chief," replied Jimmy reasonably as he used his phone to photograph the corkscrew and altar.

"Heaven forbid they should show some initiative," grumbled Shadow under his breath. He began pacing around the chapel. Today the cool air inside was welcome after the heat out on the moor, but there were a couple of paraffin heaters standing in one corner for chillier days. In many ways it was an ideal location for the duke and his guests to take a break, but he couldn't see anywhere a murderer could have hidden in the sparse interior.

"Hey, do you think they hire this place out for weddings, Chief?" asked Jimmy, who was peering out of one of the arched glassless windows. Shadow looked at him incredulously.

"I thought Sophie wanted a winter wedding. There's only half a roof here; all your guests would end up with pneumonia."

"Yeah, I guess you're right and Sophie does have her heart set on the Minster, but it is pretty here, and it's got great views down to the village. It's a shame so many abbeys and churches are ruined. Do you think they'll ever be restored? I suppose it would cost too much."

Shadow frowned as his sergeant chattered on about churches and weddings. He was thinking about something Bet and Seb had told him. He fished the map out of his pocket and spread it across the stone altar. Then with his glasses perched on his nose he tried to locate the chapel. He ran his finger from the village along the road towards the moor, then he spotted it. The site of the chapel was marked with a cross and as he had hoped there was a dash and dotted line leading back towards the road.

"Have you found something, Chief?" asked Jimmy, wandering over.

"Do you remember Seb and Plum saying the estate was riddled with tunnels like the one between the pub and the church? Well, there's one here," explained Shadow, stabbing the map with his finger. Jimmy peered at the line, then stared around the chapel.

"Where do you think the entrance is? I've got Greenwood's number. Do you want me to call him and ask him to come back?"

Shadow shook his head. "No, let's try and find it ourselves first. If we are right and the tunnel is how the murderer got here, we don't want to alert them and if we are wrong, nobody needs to know we wasted our time. You stay in here. See if you can find a trapdoor or something and I'll go and look outside."

Shadow squinted and shielded his eyes as he stepped back out into the bright sunlight and began to make his way around the chapel. Thick ivy covered most of the walls and the surrounding grass was overgrown. When he arrived on the other side of the building, he found the remains of a graveyard. There was a crumbling stone cross and several headstones that had toppled over. The few that remained upright were so badly weathered that it was almost impossible to read the carved inscriptions. He ran his fingers over the rough stone of one and managed to make out the name Greenwood. It seemed that the gamekeeper's family had been in Kirkdale almost as long as the duke's. Glancing around he wondered if this was the final resting place of any of his own ancestors.

Then his eyes settled on a large headstone that looked like it was propped against the chapel wall. He couldn't make out the dates, but the name was quite clear: DeVere. Why would a member of the DeVere family be buried here and not in the village church? He took a couple of steps forward and noticed the grass in front of this headstone had been flattened down.

"Jimmy, come here," he shouted and a few seconds later his sergeant dashed around the corner.

"Have you found the entrance, Chief?"

"Possibly. I think it's behind there," explained Shadow gesturing towards the headstone, "but I'm going to need your help to shift it."

"No problem, but shouldn't we put these on first?" asked Jimmy as he fished two pairs of blue forensic gloves from his pocket.

"I suppose so," agreed Shadow reluctantly, then when his hands were appropriately clad in latex: "Okay, you take that side. I'll push and you pull."

He put his hands of the edge of the large stone and braced himself, but as soon as he began to push the stone swung forward with ease. He was so surprised that he almost fell into the opening the stone had revealed.

"Wow you were right, Chief!" exclaimed Jimmy. "Look, the stone's been made into a door. It's on hinges."

"And it's not a stone," replied Shadow, who could now see the other side of the door, "it's wood with the outer side covered in some sort of plaster to make it look like a grave marker." He peered more closely at the hinges on Jimmy's side of the door. They were old and rusted, but also glistening in the sun. Shadow ran his finger along one, then raised it to his nose and sniffed.

"What is it?" asked Jimmy.

"WD40. They've been oiled and recently."

Together the two detectives stared into the opening the door had revealed. Despite the bright sunshine it was difficult to see what was inside. Jimmy leaned further in and shone a light on to what appeared to be narrow stone steps leading down into the earth.

"Where did you get a torch from?" asked Shadow in surprise.

"It's on my phone. Yours has one too. Look, I'll show you."

Shadow handed over his phone. Jimmy fiddled with it for a second before handing it back with the torch turned on.

"Finally, it does something useful," grunted Shadow. "Come on then, let's see what's down there."

Jimmy hesitated and pulled a face.

"You don't think there are any bats down there, do you?" he asked.

"I thought you wanted to encounter more wildlife," tutted Shadow, shaking his head in despair.

"Not bats! I don't like the way they aim for your head," Jimmy replied with a shudder.

"You've watched too many horror films. I'm more worried about us getting stuck down there. Make sure you prop the door open with something," ordered Shadow as he cautiously made his way down the roughly hewn steps. There were only six, then they stopped and there was a long tunnel ahead. Slowly he began to edge his way along. The tunnel was made of limestone. Water dripped down the walls forming shallow pools here and there on the floor. The air was cold and damp. He could hear the soft thud of Jimmy's footsteps behind him and then a bleeping sound.

"I don't believe it. You can still get a signal down here," said Jimmy.

"That'll be handy if this place caves in on our heads. Anything important?"

"A text from Ben asking us to call him about the gun. Do you want to do it now, Chief?"

"No, wait until we've finished here. We might need them to come out and take a look."

They continued to make slow progress. The tunnel was so low Shadow had to stoop and Jimmy was almost bent double in some sections. He banged his head twice.

"I guess people were shorter back when they built this." He sighed, rubbing his bruised forehead. "It must have taken them ages."

"I don't think it was built. I think it was formed naturally by an underground stream carving its way through the limestone over thousands of years," replied Shadow as he stepped over yet another puddle. "The local farmers must have known all about it and decided to use it during the years of religious persecution. I bet it goes right under the moor and they tapped into it, so to speak. We're lucky it's summer or there could be a lot more water down here."

"Where do you think it leads to, Chief?" asked Jimmy.

"I'm hoping it goes back to the road. That's the direction we set off in. How far would you say it was?"

"I don't know—about half a mile at a guess?"

"Normally that should take about ten or fifteen minutes to walk. How long have we been going?"

Jimmy looked at the screen of his phone.

"Ben's text arrived eleven minutes ago, so we should nearly be there."

"Have you still got a signal?"

"Yep. The murderer could easily have phoned or messaged Flynn from down here."

"That's what I'm starting to think," replied Shadow, then he paused. The wall he had been running his hand along to help him find his way seemed to be veering off to the right. He took a few more steps, then cursed as his shin hit something hard. He shone the thin beam of light from his phone down and realised he'd bumped into a step. Swinging the torch to the right he could see the tunnel continuing but getting lower and narrower. Looking up he thought he could see a chink of daylight.

"I think we are there," he said and began to climb the steps.

"Is there another door?" asked Jimmy. Shadow stretched out his hand and felt rough wood in front of him. He pushed and this door swung open easily, just like the other one. Blinking as he was suddenly dazzled by a shaft of sunlight, he felt something cool, smooth and waxy against his skin. Leaves. He began pushing his way forward.

"It's overgrown with ivy," he said as he managed to force his way through and out into the daylight. Jimmy emerged a few seconds later.

"It's not poison ivy is it, Chief?" he asked brushing leaves off his shoulders and out of his hair.

"Not in this country. Try reading that book of yours," grunted Shadow. He looked around him. The twisted branches of ivy were covering a narrow gap in the high stone wall that marked the edge of the castle grounds.

"Where are we anyway?" asked Jimmy.

"At the killer's point of entrance and exit by the look of things." Shadow pointed to their left. They were about a hundred yards from the entrance to the track that led up to the moors. "Let's walk back to the car along the road," Shadow suggested. "I don't fancy going through that tunnel again. Call forensics out." He was just about to step off the verge and on to the road when Jimmy grabbed hold of him.

"Stop! Careful, Chief, don't take another step," he said urgently pointing to something black in the long grass. Shadow froze with his foot poised in mid-air then slowly lowered it back to its original place as Jimmy dropped to his knees and parted the grass. Lying there, almost hidden, was a mobile phone.

"Does it still work?" asked Shadow. Jimmy carefully picked it up by the edges with his latex-gloved fingers and peered at it.

"It doesn't look damaged, but I think the battery might have run out," he said, then with his other hand rummaged through his pocket until, like a magician, he produced a small evidence bag and slipped the phone into it.

"That's another thing for Ben and Ollie to take a look at. You stay here and check there isn't anything else in the grass. I'll head back to the car and call for support," said Shadow as he made an ungainly leap from where he was standing on to the road.

Within ten minutes several uniformed officers from Easingwold were on the scene and immediately began taping off the chapel and the entrance to the tunnel, and a little over an hour later Ben and Ollie arrived too.

"What can you tell me about the gun and FitzAllan's phones?" demanded Shadow before the forensics team had even closed their car doors. "Your message left out half the information."

Ben and Ollie exchanged a wary glance before Ollie replied.

"Well, Chief, some of the team back in the incident room are going through all the calls and messages. The last message he got was from the only number he seemed to use the burner for, but it was sent to his normal phone, the smashed one. It said, 'Call me. I need to talk to you.' That was the message he was responding to when he was killed. It was sent at one twenty-four. He called back at one thirty-eight, but nobody answered."

"And then he was killed." Shadow sighed. "Jimmy said there was another number that contacted him on the burner too."

"Yes, but only once on the day before he died. It was a text and it said, 'Back out now and it will be LP who suffers.'"

"LP?" repeated Jimmy who was busy taking notes.

"Yes," confirmed Ollie, "but we don't know who or what that is."

"And the gun?" asked Shadow, failing to hide his frustration. At the moment, his colleagues were presenting him with more questions than answers.

"No not yet, Chief," Ben began apologetically. "When we found out about the lead shot, we thought the Lumley might not have been the weapon used. We were going to start looking into it but then we got called out to Tadcaster Road. Uniform found the weapon that was used to hit O'Doyle over the head."

"And?"

"It was a horseshoe," said Ollie. "Small and curved just like Sophie had described. It's quite an old one though and weighs about four pounds, so heavier than the modern ones. We ran the tests. No fingerprints, but traces of blood that match the victim's."

"Where was it found? Why was it missed last night?" demanded Shadow.

"Last night the search was focused on the bin bags and the pub car park. The horseshoe was found on the other side of the road, on the edge of the racecourse. Without Sophie's description, the search team might not have considered it a weapon," said Ben.

"It seems a weird choice. Who carries a horseshoe around with them?" asked Jimmy.

"They didn't need to," explained Ben. "The door to the pub is surrounded by them. Somebody had obviously helped themselves to one and waited for Aidan O'Doyle to come out. I checked with the girl working behind the bar. She confirmed one was missing. There should have been twenty-one and now there are only twenty. Apparently, it's an old tradition that if anyone finds a loose shoe on the Knavesmire they can bring it to the pub and exchange it for a free drink. Then the shoe is added to the entrance—you know how they are meant to bring good luck."

"I guess that horseshoe wasn't so lucky for Aidan O'Doyle." Ollie laughed.

"Or for George," snapped Shadow. "I really don't think it's something to joke about."

"Sorry, Chief," mumbled Ollie, who had turned bright red.

Shadow turned away, ignoring the exchange of raised eyebrows between Jimmy and the forensics team. He was aware he was being even more short-tempered than usual and not only because of the heat. George was relying on them and so far they had found very little to help his case. What was worse, Shadow had the distinct feeling that those involved in the two cases, both at the stable yard and the castle, were closing ranks, but that the police weren't banding together to protect one of their own in the same way and it upset him.

"Sergeant Chang, we are leaving," he announced, then pointing to Ben and Ollie: "Go over that chapel and tunnel with a fine-tooth comb." Then as Jimmy handed over the mobile they'd found: "I want a report first thing in the morning. And find out what's going on with all these damn phones."

WHEN THEY ARRIVED back at the station late that afternoon, Shadow was relieved to hear that the chief constable had returned to Northallerton. He was less pleased to find that she had emailed him and then had the email printed off and left on his desk, so he couldn't claim not to have read it. In it, she informed him that she would be returning to York in the morning and insisted he report to her before in her words 'acting rashly' in the FitzAllan case. Shadow screwed up the print-out and tossed it into the bin. He didn't know whether he was more irritated that she was breathing down his neck or that she had failed to mention Aidan's case, the outcome of which affected one of her officers.

To make matters worse he discovered that under the chief constable's instructions two incident rooms had been set up rather than one. Apparently, she didn't consider the fact that two men who worked together and were killed on the same day was enough to link the crimes.

"Start liaising with both teams and collating any evidence that overlaps then report back," he ordered Jimmy, "and get Tom to come and see me." His sergeant hurried out of his office and Shadow had just enough time to locate an indigestion tablet before Tom knocked on his door.

"You wanted to see me, sir?" he asked.

"Yes, come and sit down. Tell me what happened when you spoke to the Irish police and O'Doyle's brother."

"Like I told Sergeant Chang, his brother hadn't seen Aidan for years. They exchanged Christmas and birthday cards but that's about it. Aidan left pretty quickly over twenty years ago and has never been back. The town he and Flynn grew up in was on the border with Northern Ireland and quite a few of his friends were prominent loyalists. His brother didn't say what happened. It sounded like he was involved in something a bit dodgy, and it was Flynn who used his connections over here in the UK to get him out, then when Flynn set up his stables, he gave Aidan a job. That's not all though, sir. Apparently, Mrs FitzAllan—Siobhan—wasn't very happy when Aidan started working with Flynn. It seems her politics were very different to his. When she was younger, she was quite outspoken for her support of a united Ireland. I've been looking online and there are pictures of her with several republican politicians, some of whom were later jailed."

Shadow put his head in his hands and groaned.

"This case is already complicated enough. Please don't tell me counterterrorism are about to descend upon us."

Tom's face crinkled in confusion. "I wouldn't have thought so, sir. It all happened ages ago."

Shadow smiled ruefully. The young constable's reaction perfectly illustrated the generation gap. Shadow could clearly remember when the Troubles dominated the news and the terrorist threats when he worked at the Met, but to someone Tom's age, born not long before the Good Friday Agreement, it must seem like ancient history.

"There is something else though," Tom added. "I thought I'd take a look on social media and see what people were saying about what happened to FitzAllan and O'Doyle. Loads of horse racing fans were saying how sorry they were, but someone called Clancy Kelly had set up a whole page, kind of like a memorial full of pictures of the two men."

"That's Flynn's secretary. She works at the stables," explained Shadow.

"Well lots of people clicked that they liked it, adding heart emojis and that sort of thing, you know, sir."

"Not really but carry on, Constable."

"One name stood out: Plum DeVere. Well, I know that's the family name of the Dukes of Kirkdale, so I clicked on her page."

"And," asked Shadow who was beginning to wonder if Tom had been taking lessons from Jimmy on how to take as long as possible to pass on information.

"Well, I scrolled through her friends and a couple of names stood out. Russell James and Darren Cleeves. Both are pretty violent animal rights activists. They attacked members of one of the local hunts because they thought they were still chasing foxes not drag hunting. It was quite a nasty attack. Both of them were done for GBH. I was on duty down in custody when they were arrested last year. They're still inside, but Plum obviously knows some dodgy characters." He shrugged. "I just thought it might be worth mentioning."

"Yes, you're right. It's something to bear in mind." He nodded, adding as an afterthought, "Good work, Constable."

He turned around in his chair and began searching for the map of Kirkdale he'd folded in his coat pocket and then pushed it across the desk towards Tom.

"Take a look at this. I roughly worked out the shortest distance between Kirkdale and the Lucky Horseshoe to be twelve or thirteen miles. See if you can get something more accurate, use one of those computer programmes or apps that Sergeant Chang's always talking about. There must be one that works out the distance as the crow flies."

Tom looked up from the notes he was scribbling down. "As the crow flies, sir?"

"Yes, you know the shortest route, across fields, not necessarily following roads. Then when you've done that check all the CCTV from Tadcaster Road out to Askham Bar for any signs of a horse."

"A horse, sir?"

"Is there an echo in here?" snapped Shadow.

"Sorry, sir," said Tom. "I'll get right on to it." He was almost through the door when he stopped and looked back. "I was just wondering, sir, if there is any news about Sergeant Hedley—you know if he's holding up okay?"

"I plan on going to see him tomorrow. I'll let you know," replied Shadow.

Tom nodded and gave a weak smile. "Thanks, sir."

When the young constable had disappeared, Shadow leaned back in his chair and closed his eyes. His head was beginning to throb with all the information swirling around inside. He was considering slipping out and taking a walk down by the river when he heard the sound of trainer-clad feet hurrying down the corridor.

"Yes, Sergeant," he called out as he reluctantly opened his eyes to see Jimmy standing in the doorway, looking particularly pleased with himself.

"We got it, Chief. A definite connection between the two deaths."

"Come in and shut the door then," said Shadow. Jimmy slid into the chair opposite him.

"Okay, so I spoke to both teams, particularly those working on the burner phones, and it was there straight away.

The number that sent a text to FitzAllan about 'LP' and the one that told O'Doyle to meet them outside is the same."

Shadow exhaled loudly with relief. "Finally, we're getting somewhere," he said. "That's it. From now on the two incident rooms merge. I'll sort out any problems with the chief constable."

"I'll get on to it, Chief."

"How long before we can trace the owner of the phone?"

"We need to wait for forensics, Chief. Hey, who do you think LP is? Lady Plum?" asked Jimmy. "Opposites attract and all that."

"Possibly." Shadow sighed. "Although let me check something for a second." He reached over for the copy of *Debrett's* he'd been driving around with all day, flicked through and ran his finger down the page. "There, I thought so—Lavinia Eastwold's middle name is Patricia. LP."

Jimmy pulled a face at this idea. "I don't think so, Chief. By all accounts Flynn was a lady killer. Why would he go for her? And I can't see her being involved with a lowly horse trainer, she's too much of a snob," said Jimmy.

Shadow nodded. "You're probably right. We'll keep looking into it," he agreed then paused as he thought. "LP might not even be the mystery woman. It could be a horse. Check and see if there are any with those initials at FitzAllan's stables."

"Will do, Chief. By the way, what did Tom have to report?"

"Nothing much, only that on top of everything else we might need to start investigating animal rights activists and Irish terrorists." Shadow sighed as he stood up and pulled on his coat. Then noting Jimmy's confused expression, said, "Never mind, Sergeant. Get Tom to fill you in. I'm going now, but I'll be back here bright and early tomorrow morning. Double-check the gun licences for everyone who was shooting with FitzAllan and don't forget to see if anyone at the stables or any of the castle staff have got a record. The way things are going it wouldn't surprise me if Jarvis turned out to be an international jewel thief."

WHEN HE LEFT the station, Shadow went for a quiet stroll through Dean's Park to clear his head, so it was late when he finally arrived at La Scuola Femminile, one of his favourite Italian restaurants. The place was heaving with racegoers, but his usual table by the window was still waiting for him. There was no sign of the owners Francesco and Lucia; instead their son, Marco, greeted him warmly and showed him to his seat.

"Where are your mum and dad?" asked Shadow.

"My granny has been staying with us, but she started feeling dizzy earlier, so Mum and Dad have taken her to the hospital to get her checked over. I told them I'd be able to manage," explained the young man.

"And can you?"

"Almost," replied Marco with a smile. Shadow ordered a mixed seafood starter, followed by the sea bass and a bottle of Grillo to accompany it. Then he settled back in his chair to consider the case. The gun used to shoot FitzAllan was a puzzle, as were the number of mobile phones, but what he was really struggling with was a motive. Logic told him the answer must involve racehorses somehow, but this business of FitzAllan's possible infidelity was bothering him. He took a sip of wine and sincerely hoped Tom's information about the two men's pasts wasn't going to lead the investigation back to Ireland. That would surely delay things and for George's sake, Shadow wanted to solve this case as soon as possible.

Less than an hour later, he pushed his knife and fork together having demolished the sea bass and sautéed potatoes with almost indecent haste. He leaned back in his chair with a satisfied sigh, when he noticed Marco nervously waiting to speak to him.

"Is something wrong?" he asked quietly.

"I'm sorry to bother you, Chief Inspector, but I don't know what to do?" The young man looked and sounded worried. "Lord Eastwold is in the private dining room. The rest of his party left, but he stayed behind drinking. He's quite far gone. His waiter gave him the bill to settle but his credit card has been declined. When we told him, he got quite angry. Normally, we would call the police, but his friends and family are good customers, and Mum and Dad wouldn't want any bad publicity."

Shadow sympathised with his predicament. Even when sober and talking to a senior police officer, Eastwold had come across as rude and belligerent. God knows what he was like when he was drunk. Shadow stood up.

"I'll go through and have a quiet word with Lord Eastwold and see if that helps," he said.

"Oh, thank you, Chief Inspector," replied the young man, visibly relieved.

"Did the rest of the party leave through the main door?" asked Shadow, wondering how he had missed seeing any of them.

"No there's a side door in the private dining room that leads across the garden and out on to the Minster Plaza," explained Marco.

Shadow followed him through the restaurant to the private dining room, which was situated in a conservatory with beautiful views of the floodlit Minster. In the centre of the room, a large glass table was still covered in the debris of what must have been a dinner for a party of twelve, but now there was only one solitary diner remaining. Lord Eastwold had removed his jacket and tie and his feet were resting on one of the other chairs. In one hand was a fat cigar and in the other he was holding a glass of what looked like brandy.

"Good evening, Lord Eastwold," said Shadow. The lord looked up and narrowed his eyes as he tried to focus on who was addressing him.

"Not you again. What do you want?" he replied in a slurred voice.

"I understand there was a problem with your credit card."

"Bloody banks, who the hell do they think they are? There's nothing wrong with my credit. I'll call in and settle up some time tomorrow," he declared as he waved his cigar around airily.

"I'm afraid that won't be possible, sir. Do you have any other cards or another way to settle the bill?"

Lord Eastwold began patting his pockets and shaking his jacket in an exaggerated fashion and finally produced his cheque book that had been folded in half.

"Here we are I'll write you a good old-fashioned cheque. How's that?"

"We haven't been paid by cheque for years," whispered Marco, who was hovering behind Shadow with the bill. Shadow handed the bill over to Lord Eastwold and winced when he saw the total was almost a thousand pounds. He watched as Eastwold struggled to focus as he slowly began to write, then when he'd finished, he checked the date, amount and signature before handing it to Marco.

"I know it's not ideal, but it's better than nothing and at least if it does bounce, he'll be easy enough to find. It's either this or I can call uniform in," offered Shadow.

Marco shook his head. "No, Sir Charles Richmond—the

MP—was in the party. He's one of our best customers. Mum and Dad wouldn't want to do anything that might embarrass him."

"I'm sure they'll be happy with the way you've handled the situation," Shadow said as he patted Marco on the shoulder and then hauled his lordship to his feet.

"Time to go I think, sir."

Fortunately, Lord Eastwold didn't argue and together they staggered out through the private dining room door and across the small walled garden with Marco following close behind. His lordship continued talking loudly along the way.

"You know, Shadow my good man, in a few days all my problems will be solved. They'll disappear in a heartbeat." He seemed to be highly amused by this last comment and began laughing loudly, then he pointed to Marco. "Never fear, young man. Tomorrow evening I shall return to your excellent establishment and celebrate with your finest champagne."

"Oh God, please don't," said Marco under his breath as he held the garden gate open for Shadow, before shaking his hand.

"I can't thank you enough for your help, Chief Inspector."

"No problem at all, Marco. Don't worry, everything will be fine and if it isn't let me know."

Out in the plaza, the cool evening air seemed to sober Lord Eastwold up a little, at least enough so he no longer needed Shadow to support him.

"Thank you, my good man," he slurred as he clapped Shadow on the back. Then he walked unsteadily towards a taxi that had just dropped a fare off on Duncombe Place. Shadow watched him climb into the taxi and hoped for the driver's sake he wasn't sick on the way home.

It was still too warm and muggy to sleep when he returned to *Florence*, so he opened a bottle of Chianti and went to sit outside and mull over the case a little more. It had been a long day of interviews and as always after receiving so much information it took a while to understand which bits were important. He imagined it was like panning for gold. He had to sift through an awful lot of rubbish to find a few precious nuggets.

Perhaps because they had been more forthcoming, he found himself dwelling on comments some of the women had made. Siobhan describing Aidan as being sprawled across the road was still stuck in his mind. Then there was Lavinia's barely disguised jealousy of Annabel, and not providing any real reason for turning up late to the shoot. Plum had also been less than subtle when it came to her desire that Seb should inherit the estate, but none of this seemed to link back to Flynn. Something else that was troubling him, was despite almost every female he spoke to telling him how attractive Flynn was, he was no closer to discovering who he had been having an affair with.

As Shadow sipped his wine, he watched as his neighbours

the geese flew low under Skeldergate Bridge and landed with much honking on the river, sending a shower of water splashing on to the boat.

"Bloody hooligans," he muttered wiping his face dry with the back of his hand. Then knocking back the last of the Chianti in the glass, he remembered something else. The previous day Annabel had told Bertie she couldn't wear her white dress because it had been stained by wine. Lavinia said Annabel didn't drink, so who had spilt the wine on her? Bertie or her brother, or was it possible that she had been the one to throw wine over Flynn and have it splash on to her? He wasn't sure, but he would very much like to have seen that white dress.

For once he didn't feel like pouring himself a second glass and decided to go to bed instead. Between the stains on Flynn's shirt, Annabel's dress and the carpet stains in Clancy's cottage he'd had enough wine for one night.

CHAPTER SEVEN

Across 6. Tim and Tom begin to put money on who they think will win (7 letters)

T HE NEXT MORNING when, Shadow bought his *Yorkshire Post* from the newsagent's as usual, he noticed the headlines in one of the tabloids: 'Racing Death Mystery—Trainer killed on shoot with Duke and MP'. Alongside the story, there were small photos of Flynn, Bertie and Sir Charles, but the main picture was of a pouting Annabel, from her modelling days. Immediately, Shadow remembered seeing Eastwold slipping the brown envelope into his pocket. Giles Greenwood had been wrong. Someone in the village had talked.

It was before nine when he arrived in the incident room. He wanted to have as much information as possible before being grilled by the chief constable. Jimmy was already there sipping one of his expensive takeaway coffees.

"Morning, Chief," he said, then seeing the newspaper Shadow had brought with him: "Oh dear they won't be very happy with that headline up at Kirkdale Castle."

"No," agreed Shadow, "I doubt the chief constable will

be either."

"I've got good news though. Siobhan, Bertie and Piers each have a fairly long list of motoring offences against their names, but none of the castle staff or anyone at the stables has a criminal record," Jimmy said cheerfully. Shadow was about to reply that he didn't think this was particularly good news when Ben and Ollie dashed into the room, out of breath. Their appearance was even more chaotic than usual. Ben's shirt was untucked, and Ollie was still tying his tie.

"Sorry, Chief, we both overslept. Are we late?" panted Ben as he tried to flatten down his hair.

"Almost," muttered Shadow. "What else did you find yesterday? Anything in the chapel or tunnel? Where there any prints on the phone we found? Could you trace it? Did Jimmy tell you the same number called both O'Doyle and FitzAllan?" He could hear himself firing questions around like a machine gun, but the disorganised scientists had the uncanny ability to make him more impatient than ever.

"Well," began Ollie, "firstly nothing in the chapel, but it's possible the killer was never in there. We didn't find prints on the entrance to the tunnel and no footprints either."

"It's so wet down there we didn't really expect to find any," added Ben.

"Right," agreed Ollie, "but re the phone you found—we've managed to charge it by the way—it had a great thumbprint on it, but no match on the database. Again, not that we were expecting to find any."

Shadow leaned against the desk he was standing next to and folded his arms. He should never have insisted on meeting them himself. He should have sent Jimmy to listen to what they hadn't found and only report back if they actually said something that was worth repeating.

"But the tunnel phone is the number that FitzAllan used his burner phone to contact and the number that called him on his usual phone before he died," Ollie continued.

"Is it registered to anyone?" asked Jimmy, who was better at reading his boss's body language than his two colleagues.

"No, it's a burner," replied Ben.

"What about the number that called O'Doyle and FitzAllan the day before he died?" asked Shadow.

"That's a burner too."

"For crying out loud," Shadow exclaimed in exasperation. "Why haven't these damned things been banned yet? Who needs to use one unless they are up to no good?"

"Actually, Chief." Ollie raised his hand, ignoring Jimmy who was silently shaking his head at him. "I believe the Home Office has raised the possibility of making them illegal."

"But if they did criminals will only use encrypted internet phone services like WhatsApp, and these disposable phones can be useful for someone who doesn't want to get tied into a contract," said Ben.

Shadow raised his eyes to the ceiling.

"All right, all right, let's move on from phones. What about the gun used to kill FitzAllan? Was it the Lumley or not?"

Ollie and Ben exchanged a worried glance.

"Yes, at least we think so, but we don't know how," said Ben hesitantly.

"What?" Shadow really didn't think he had any more patience left to lose.

"Well, you see it only uses special Lumley cartridges and they don't fit any other gun. FitzAllan had plenty containing the modern steel pellets, but the ones found in him are the older lead version. We've run some tests and carried out some research and they are about fifty years old," explained Ben.

Shadow's brow creased. "So, you are telling me either the killer had another of these extremely rare and valuable guns or they somehow managed to get FitzAllan's gun off him, load it with fifty-year-old cartridges, and then shoot him with it twice?"

"When you put it like that, I know it doesn't sound very plausible," said Ben.

"Plausible? It sounds impossible," snapped Shadow as he stood up and pointed to Ollie. "All right, you can go and speak to Dr Donaldson and even if you need to beg him on bended knee to examine the body again, make sure he's one hundred per cent certain FitzAllan wasn't hit on the head or incapacitated in some way before he died."

Then he turned to Ben. "You said you knew about guns. If these Lumleys are as special as you say, there must be an expert who can tell you how many there are in the country and who has them," he said as he swung his arm out and pointed to the door.

"Yes, Chief," they replied in unison, before scurrying away. When they had disappeared, Shadow turned back to Jimmy.

"I swear they'll be the death of me. What do we have on the CCTV from the racecourse and on Tadcaster Road?" asked Shadow.

Jimmy began scrolling through his notes. "Plenty of images of Siobhan at the racecourse all afternoon and driving off in her horsebox at the time she told us. Not long after she'd gone, Aidan showed up on the camera at the entrance to the course. It looks like that's when he headed across the road to the Lucky Horseshoe."

"Doesn't the pub have a camera?"

"Yes, but it only covers the car park at the back, not the side entrance Aidan used."

"And nothing on any of the other cameras in the area. No sign of a horse?"

"I'm afraid not, Chief, but Tom left a message. He did some calculations and agreed with you that it would take a couple of hours there and back from Kirkdale to York cross-country on a horse."

Right on cue Tom appeared.

"Morning, sir, we've just received a message from the chief constable's office. She's been held up at HQ and won't be here until later this afternoon."

"There is a God," said Shadow exhaling loudly as he stood up. "Right, in that case, I'm off to see how George is doing. Jimmy, you keep looking into the stables. See if FitzAllan has ever been involved in anything underhand, using performance-enhancing drugs, that sort of thing. And keep chasing our friends in forensics for information. I don't want them getting distracted and see if you can find out anything about Lord Eastwold's financial position."

Jimmy looked up from scribbling all the instructions down. "Anything else, Chief?"

"Yes," replied Shadow. "Tom, I want you to find out as much information as you can about the previous Duke of Kirkdale, particularly his time in the army serving in Northern Ireland. Then see if you can get hold of a plan of Kirkdale Castle or architectural drawings. It must be registered as a listed building or a building of historic importance. See what you can get your hands on."

Without any further explanation Shadow left the incident room and the station and made his way across St Helen's Square. On his way to George's, he decided to call into La Scuola Femminile to see if Marco had encountered any problems paying Lord Eastwold's cheque in at the bank. He glanced at his watch. It was about an hour before they were due to open for lunch; however, as he turned on to

Petergate he saw Sir Charles already leaving the restaurant.

"Hello there, Chief Inspector," said the politician. He was immaculately dressed as always in a navy pinstriped suit and his gold badge for the members' enclosure at the racecourse was dangling from the top button of his jacket.

"Morning, Sir Charles, are you off to the races again to-day?"

"Yes, I'm on my way now. I have a meeting with the stewards before lunch." He turned and nodded towards La Scuola Femminile. "I understand Eastwold made rather a fool of himself after we'd left last night. I've just called in and settled the bill. Between you and me, I didn't have much faith in Eastwold's cheque clearing and after the shooting Annabel doesn't need any more grief."

"How did you know about him paying by cheque?"

"It was me who paid for his taxi when he arrived back at Kirkdale. Everyone else had gone to bed. Of course, he didn't have any cash and I had to hear all about the terrible banks and how he couldn't pay his bill here either. Thank you for stepping in by the way. As I said the last thing Annabel needed is to bail her brother-in-law out."

"Well, it was good of you to come over. I'm sure Marco appreciated it."

"Not at all, I should have known better than to leave Eastwold to settle up."

The two men shook hands and Shadow watched as the member of parliament disappeared down Petergate, then he turned and entered the restaurant. He found a relieved-looking Marco at the reception desk, tearing up Eastwold's cheque.

"We'll never know if it would have bounced or not now," said Shadow. Marco looked up and grinned.

"No thankfully. Sir Charles phoned this morning and asked me not to present it to the bank. He said he'd call in and settle the bill and he just did. Cash too."

"Even better," replied Shadow. "By the way, when did Sir Charles leave last night?"

"About an hour before Lord Eastwold. Lord Eastwold was already quite drunk, and his wife and sister seemed a bit upset, so Sir Charles said he would take them both home."

"Where was the Duke of Kirkdale? Wasn't he here with them all?"

"No, there was no sign of him."

"Well at least everything has worked out okay. How's your granny by the way?"

"Good thanks, Chief Inspector. They kept her in over-night to run some tests but she's coming out later today."

"More good news. Give your parents my regards."

With a wave goodbye Shadow left, wondering why Sir Charles was so concerned for Annabel DeVere. His interest seemed more than that of a gracious guest. He headed down Goodramgate and then Monkgate, before turning towards Heworth where George lived in a neat and tidy semi-detached house overlooking the stray.

"It's good of you to come, John," said Carol as she answered the door. "Is there any news?" Her voice sounded both hopeful and fearful.

Shadow stepped into the hallway. "Nothing concrete yet, but everyone is doing all they can," he reassured her. "How is he?"

"Putting on a brave face for my benefit." She sighed. "I wish he wouldn't." She showed Shadow through to the living room. Like the hallway it was spotlessly clean and there was a faint smell of baking wafting through from the kitchen. Wherever he looked there were framed photos of Carol and George's two daughters, from their school days, through to university graduations and their weddings. Sitting in pride of place on the mantelpiece was a large picture of Harry, their grandson. At one end of the room a sofa and two armchairs were arranged around a fireplace with a gas fire and at the other end was a dining table and chairs that George seemed to have commandeered. He stood up when he saw Shadow and shook his hand warmly.

"I'll leave you two to chat while I go and put the kettle on," announced Carol before disappearing into the kitchen.

"It looks like you are keeping yourself busy," commented Shadow as he sat down and took in the piles of notebooks, and pens and papers stacked in front of George.

"I've been going through my old diaries. I've found the one from the year you joined us. I think you might find it interesting, especially with this investigation at the Kirkdale estate. Do you remember old Maurice Hardwick? I couldn't sleep last night, and I remembered he knew your father. When you arrived at the station, I wrote down what he told me." George put his glasses on and cleared his throat before he began reading. "He began by saying you seemed a bit quiet and reserved, but that if you were even half the officer your dad had been, you'd be all right."

"It's kind of you to think of me, George," interrupted Shadow gently. He was truly touched his old friend had been thinking of him, but he should be concentrating on his own case. George put up his hand to stop him.

"Nonsense. I need to do something to keep my mind off things. Carol thinks I'm barmy, but the truth is I miss my files, my office. I miss being useful. Now listen to the next bit. Sergeant Hardwick told me your dad was shot by a Lumley gun, but they never found it." He looked up with a triumphant expression. "So, don't you think it strange that a Lumley gun should be used in a shooting in the same village again fifty-odd years later?"

"Very odd," murmured Shadow as he tried to process what his friend was telling him. George looked disappointed by his less than enthusiastic reaction. He removed his glasses and rubbed his eyes.

"I don't know, John, maybe I am past it and maybe I'm being an old fool, but what if the Lumley gun FitzAllan had was the same one that killed your dad?"

"Hold on," said Shadow suddenly, "how do you know

what sort of gun was used in the FitzAllan shooting?"

"Ben from forensics phoned me from the crime scene late that afternoon. He said it was an unusual gun and asked me if I had any information in the records office. It was the last thing I was researching before I left that night. What do you think?"

Shadow's first reaction was to feel a pang of guilt. Ben had started looking into the Lumley already; perhaps he'd been a bit harsh on him at their meeting this morning. His forehead creased as he recalled the few details he knew of his father's death.

"The gun was never recovered."

"No." George shook his head. "Identified from the cartridges found in the wood but there was no sign of the gun. That's what I was looking up. When you arrived old Sarge Hardwick told me there was something fishy about the investigation. Considering it involved the death of one of our own, it wasn't very thorough. Privately Sarge Hardwick wondered if there had been a cover-up."

"Which officer was leading the investigation?" asked Shadow.

"Grunwell," replied George. "He was only a DI back then but…"

George hesitated, but Shadow didn't need to hear any more. Grunwell had been a chief inspector at the station before Shadow. Since his retirement Shadow had unearthed countless previous investigations where his predecessor had acted less than professionally. He had grown used to it, but to hear Grunwell had been at best lax and at worst corrupt when he was in charge of investigating his own father's death was a shock.

"The Lumley gun FitzAllan had has been used quite openly by the DeVeres for years before he inherited it. Even with Grunwell investigating, surely they wouldn't have continued using the gun that killed my father so blatantly. And if it wasn't that gun and Lumleys are meant to be as rare and expensive as Ben tells me, how would a poacher have got his hands on one?"

"No, no it's even more complicated than that," said George, glasses perched on his nose once more as he referred to yet more notes. "On the night your father was killed, there was a break-in at Kirkdale Castle. Only in the gunroom though, and the only thing taken was one of the Lumleys. They came as a pair originally, you see. The one FitzAllan had was the one left behind."

Shadow shook his head. It didn't make any sense. If the criminal's plan was to break into the castle and steal valuable guns, why would they risk getting caught just to bag a few pheasants?

"Who reported there was a poacher?" he asked. "I was told it was the old gamekeeper's wife?"

"Yes, that's right. She phoned your dad. She said she saw a light in the woods, couldn't find her husband and called the police out instead. However, the gamekeeper did make the call to us and the ambulance when your dad was shot."

Shadow nodded. What George was telling him tallied with Bill Greenwood's story, but the old gamekeeper had failed to mention the theft from the castle gunroom.

"Was anyone else in the village involved that night?"

"No, I don't think so. The duke was away at the time. The duchess was at home and of course your mother and grandparents were informed."

Shadow nodded. He tried to imagine how they must have felt receiving that call. One of his few memories of living in the village was of his mother wearing black and the house being full of people all talking in hushed tones.

"What about the forensics report back then?" he asked. "I know it would have been more basic, but did they find any fingerprints in the castle gunroom?"

Before George could answer, Carol bustled in carrying a tray of tea and homemade shortbread biscuits.

"Oh now, George, I told you not to bother John with all that business about his poor father." She put the tray down and patted Shadow on the shoulder. "It must be difficult enough for him to be back in Kirkdale investigating another death. I think you are being very brave, love."

Shadow felt his cheeks begin to burn. "It's fine really, Carol," he insisted. "I was very young. I don't remember what happened."

Carol shook her head and smiled indulgently, as if she didn't believe him. He thought it best to change the subject.

"What's been going on with you two? Have you contacted a lawyer?"

"Cornelius Rutherford is our family solicitor," replied Carol, while George quietly sipped his tea. "He said if necessary, he'll contact a barrister in Leeds who specialises in our sort of case, if it comes to it. She's meant to be very good."

George looked up briefly.

"I know Rutherford meant to reassure me, but he made me feel worse to be honest."

"Nonsense," chided Carol, "it's best to be prepared." She paused and turned to Shadow. "Have you made any progress yet, John?" She tried her best to sound casual, but he knew how desperate they must be for news.

He put down the piece of shortbread he had been about to pop in his mouth and cleared his throat "Unfortunately no witnesses have come forward as yet, but as you said yourself there were no other cars on the road at the time of the accident. We have found the weapon used to injure O'Doyle, so that's something. Nothing as yet on the CCTV. We are looking into a lead we have on the victim's phone messages, but we haven't managed to find who was contacting him before he died, not yet anyway. But once we find who attacked him, well that should have an impact on the decision about your case." Despite his best efforts to sound upbeat, the looks of disappointment of his friends' faces told him he'd failed.

Carol attempted a weak smile. "I know you are doing everything you can," she said.

Shadow quickly drank the rest of his tea and stood up. "I should be getting back to the station and see if there's been any progress. Before I go, there was something I wanted to ask you about the night of the accident, George."

His friend's face clouded. It was clear he wanted to get back to his diaries and keep his mind off the accident.

"I don't think I've got anything else to say, John. I must have gone over it in my head a million times."

"You said you thought you saw a fox and that's why you swerved. Are you sure it was a fox? Could it have been something else?"

George paused and thought.

"It sounds stupid now, but all I really saw was a flash of colour in my lights on the edge of the racecourse. It was a lovely rusty-red colour. My first thought was—fox! I made a split-second decision, thought it was about to run out in front of me and I swerved. I've always liked them. Never understood why anyone would want to hunt them."

"So, it was on the roadside not in the road when you swerved?"

"Yes, like I said I jumped to the wrong conclusion and swerved the other way. There were no cars behind me or coming towards me, only those few bin bags. I knew I was going to hit them, but I thought at the worst I'd dent my bumper." He paused and shook his head. "How wrong I was."

Shadow turned to Carol. "Did you see it too?"

"Yes." She nodded. "But like George said, it was just a flash of colour caught in the headlights at the side of the road." She paused. "But rather than rusty red, I'd have said chestnut."

SHADOW LEFT THE house in Heworth, having promised to keep in touch. He had refused Carol's offer of lunch and instead called into the Cross Keys on Goodramgate. However, he stepped through the doors and found that the place was full of young men in shiny suits and young ladies in short skirts and big hats getting a few drinks in before they headed to the races. He promptly turned on his heel and walked out again. He didn't have much of an appetite anyway.

Perhaps Carol was right he thought as he walked slowly back up Stonegate. Maybe this case and its connection to his past was affecting him more than he'd admitted. He certainly hadn't slept well the last two nights and no doubt his colleagues would say he'd been even more irritable than usual. He was still mulling this thought over when he arrived back at the station and saw Ben hovering in reception.

"Are you waiting for me?" asked Shadow. The young scientist shifted from one foot to the other and his face had turned a deep shade of red.

"Yes, Chief. I've got some information about the gun, but I wanted to tell you face to face."

Shadow raised an eyebrow. "I see, you'd better come up to my office then."

A few minutes later they were facing each other across Shadow's desk, although the scientist was having difficulty looking the chief inspector in the eye.

"What do you have to tell me?" asked Shadow, trying not to sound impatient.

"Well, I contacted someone at the Lumley Guns head office about the gun we found with FitzAllan and he told us originally it was one of a pair. I thought it was strange, that FitzAllan was the only one shooting with a single gun. The man at Lumley's told me the police had…"

"Reported that the other one was stolen over fifty years ago from the gunroom at Kirkdale Castle," interrupted Shadow.

"You know about that?" asked Ben looking surprised.

"Yes, George has just told me. It was stolen the night my father was killed."

Ben had turned red again. "That's the bit I really wanted to talk to you about. You see we, Ollie and I, thought it was weird—you know too much of a coincidence. As George isn't around, we asked Sophie to check the records at her place and see if there was a file on the, um, on the, er, examination of your dad."

"And?"

"Well, the pellets that were found in him were the same as the ones Donaldson found in FitzAllan. Not similar, but identical. They are the old-fashioned lead ones and the cartridge caps in each batch were printed with the same serial number. The serial number on the ones found the night your dad died and on the fragment of cap we found near FitzAllan are from the same batch." He paused again. "I…well we…didn't want to tell you over the phone or incident room."

Shadow let this information sink in for a second, then he stood up and held out his hand to Ben.

"Thank you for coming to tell me in person. It was good of you. I appreciate it."

Ben rose to his feet too, looking rather taken aback. He shook Shadow's hand.

"No problem, Chief. I'll go now. Get back to the lab, see what's happening with the phones."

Shadow watched him go. Then turned his chair around and stared out of the window at the river and the racegoers in their brightly coloured outfits, laughing and joking as they trooped across Lendal Bridge. Had someone really held on to the gun and the same ammunition that killed his father all these years and then used them against FitzAllan? Could they have been hidden somewhere and found by chance? He gave his head a shake. There were too many questions and what he and more importantly George needed now were answers.

HE LEFT HIS office and went in search of Jimmy. He found his sergeant in the incident room staring intently at the screen of his phone.

"Anything to report?" he asked.

"Yes, I think I might, Chief. Hold on a second," he replied before moving over to one of the computers and tapping away at the keyboard. "You know how you had the idea of Siobhan riding her horse back here to the Lucky Horseshoe?"

"Yes, but Tom checked, and nothing showed up on the CCTV."

"I know, but I was checking up on FitzAllan—nobody has a word to say against him, by the way—then I started thinking. Seeing a horse at that time of night would be pretty unusual and so if anyone had spotted him, they might have put it on social media."

"If you say so," muttered Shadow, who didn't understand the appeal of Facebook and Twitter no matter how often Jimmy enthused about them.

"Anyway," continued his sergeant, "I did a search and found something on Instagram. Someone posted a picture of a chestnut horse on the Knavesmire the night Aidan was killed with the caption: 'Races started early for this horse.' I thought that was pretty funny and they used the hashtags #Knavesmire, #onlyinYork, and #toomanyshandies. Whoever posted it has got a great sense of humour."

"But not a steady hand. It's a bit blurred," said Shadow as he stared at the unclear picture of a chestnut horse tethered to a tree in the dark. He couldn't let himself get too carried away, but this might be the breakthrough they needed. "It looks like Carol was right."

"Chief?"

"She described the flash of colour they saw in the headlights as being chestnut. I don't think it was a fox George saw, but Parnell's tail swishing out as Siobhan rode away along the edge of the Knavesmire after she'd hit Aidan."

"That would make sense. Talk about bad timing on George's part," said Jimmy. "I was thinking maybe whoever took the photo was in a car too. That would explain the blurring. I'm going to DM them and ask them about it. They might have a clearer image."

"No," replied Shadow briskly, "let Tom do that. We shouldn't waste any time. Let's head back to Kirkdale. You go to the stables. Get as many photos as possible of Parnell. Make some excuse. Tell Clancy you need to see Flynn's diary or something."

"Should I show that picture to anyone at the stables? See if they can identify it as Parnell?"

Shadow shook his head firmly. "No, it's tempting as Siobhan won't be there—she'll be here at the races—but I don't want anyone warning her or she might do a disappearing act. While you go to the stables, I want to go and speak to Plum again and find out if she could really be LP."

As THEY DROVE through the North Yorkshire countryside yet again, Shadow told Jimmy about seeing Sir Charles and George, and about the gun and ammunition.

"So that's why Ben was looking for you. I thought he seemed nervous. You know, Chief, I've been thinking maybe we should concentrate on Ireland a bit more. Both the victims were from there and I've been working on a theory." He paused, but there was no sarcastic comment from Shadow. "So, fifty years ago things in Northern Ireland were pretty bad and there was a lot of terrorist activity. If the duke was a soldier there and high-profile, he could have been a target. Maybe some terrorists broke into the castle stole the gun, got disturbed by your dad, chased him into the wood and killed him. They held on to the gun and ammunition and then came back and used it against FitzAllan and O'Doyle. Those two could have seen something or said something they shouldn't. We know O'Doyle had to leave the country quickly. Perhaps the terrorists finally caught up with them and they were killed in revenge."

Jimmy glanced across expectantly at his boss and for once Shadow didn't dismiss his suggestion immediately. It did indeed sound like a plot for a film Jimmy might have watched, but this case seemed to be getting more complicated by the day, so instead he simply said, "Hopefully, the information Tom is finding about the late duke's time in Ireland will shed some light on his connection to FitzAllan. Did you find out anything about Eastwold?"

"Yes, I ran a check through Companies House, and he's been a director of loads of companies all of which have gone into receivership. His family estate, Eastwold Hall, is now a limited company. He's the sole director. He's taken out a second charge on the property and I'm no accountant, Chief, but the last lot of figures he filed don't look too healthy."

"No wonder he can't pay his bills and is selling stories to the tabloids."

"That was him?" asked Jimmy.

"I think so, I saw him talking to a journalist at the village pub."

"Well, that's not very loyal and when Sir Charles has just bailed him out at the restaurant as well."

"I don't think it was him Sir Charles was really helping," replied Shadow without any further elaboration.

JIMMY DROPPED HIM off at the entrance to Bluebell Farm and with his jacket now folded over his arm, Shadow crunched up the gravel drive in the blazing sun. The donkey and two goats all raised their heads and watched his progress silently for a moment before returning to chewing the grass.

Shadow approached the front door. There appeared to be no sign of human life at Bluebell Farm and Plum's ancient Volvo was missing from the yard. Undeterred Shadow rang the doorbell. It was an old-fashioned wrought-iron pulley contraption. It grated and creaked as he moved it but from somewhere deep inside the house, he could hear the distant sound of a clanging bell. A few seconds later, Seb opened the door. The young man was wearing ripped jeans and a faded rugby shirt. His feet were bare, but he still towered over Shadow.

"Hello, Chief Inspector, would you like to come in?"

"Hello, I was hoping to speak with your mother," he said as Seb led him through the farmhouse to the sitting room. It was a long thin house and the rooms all led into each other. The sitting room had a light and airy feel despite the low-beamed ceilings. The floors were red quarry tiles and covered with rugs scattered here and there. The walls were all painted white and hung with African tribal masks and brightly coloured canvases.

"Sit down, Chief Inspector. I'll go and put the kettle on. Mum's at a meeting. I don't know how long she'll be, but you are welcome to wait," said Seb as he disappeared through the doorway into the kitchen. Shadow watched the young man go. With his easy manner and need to duck his head as he stepped under the low doorframe, he reminded Shadow of Jimmy. It was hard to imagine that one day he would be sitting in the House of Lords and have all the responsibility of running the vast Kirkdale estate. Shadow sank into one of the sofas that wasn't already occupied by a snoozing cat and glanced around the room.

Amongst the squishy sofas and leather elephants, rhinos and crocodiles were several low wooden tables. On one of these tables a collection of old photos was spread out. Shadow began to look through them. Seb returned carrying a tray with two mugs of tea and a plate of chocolate biscuits. He placed it on the table in front of Shadow, who was starving having missed lunch and couldn't resist helping himself to one.

"Mum's making a montage of those," Seb said nodding towards the photos. "She found them in a box in the castle attics and she's going to give it to Granny as a present for her birthday next month."

"There's plenty to choose from. Your grandmother has certainly led an eventful life," replied Shadow as he peered at some of the images. There was one of Sybil sitting in the cockpit of a biplane, jumping a fence on a horse and another of her holding a shotgun and a trophy.

"You can say that again," said Seb with a laugh, "but she's had to slow down since her stroke last year. Then they diagnosed her with angina, so no more flying, riding or shooting. She's really pissed off about it." He flushed. "I mean extremely upset about it. She's convinced the bout of scarlet fever they all had damaged her heart as well as Uncle Bertie's."

Shadow pointed to a photo of the dowager duchess with two very familiar ladies. "Are they who I think they are?" asked Shadow.

"Yes, it was taken about thirty years ago up at Balmoral, so before my time I'm afraid," said Seb. Shadow continued to sift through the photos. As well as those showing snippets of Sybil's life, there were at least a dozen of Flynn FitzAllan with an older man; grinning together at the races or out shooting.

"Is this your grandfather?" he asked.

"Yes, he and Flynn were really close. Grandpa adored him. I maybe shouldn't say this, but he got on much better with him than he did with Uncle Bertie."

"And is this one of you?" Shadow asked, picking up another photo of a teenage boy and an older man.

"Yes, on my sixteenth birthday. I'm with Grandpa. Do you remember I told you about the one and only time he took me shooting?"

Shadow peered a little closer at the picture of the old duke with his arm proudly around his grandson.

"It's a good photo. What a shame it's been hidden away."

"Oh, you know how Mum feels about blood sports, Chief Inspector."

"Is that the Lumley gun you are holding?"

"Yes, the one Grandpa left to Flynn. He let me borrow it for the day. Not that it helped much. I was rubbish. I must take after Dad's side of the family. Granny and Grandpa were both crack shots."

"Oh well, I expect your heart wasn't in it," reasoned Shadow kindly as he took another biscuit. "Is it only you and your mum who live here?"

Seb nodded. "Yes, it's always been just the two of us since Dad died. She's had one or two boyfriends over the years, but nothing serious. I told her I wouldn't mind if she met someone, but she always says nobody could compare to Dad."

"I see," said Shadow. The more he thought about it, the less sense it made that Plum would be LP. She was single, Siobhan and Flynn's marriage was more of a business arrangement, and Seb didn't mind, so why would they need to take elaborate measures like using burner phones to hide the fact they were in a relationship? He finished his tea and stood up.

"I won't keep you any longer, Seb. I'll catch up with your mum another time. Thanks for the tea."

SHADOW HAD ARRANGED to meet Jimmy outside the church and his sergeant was already waiting for him.

"Well?"

Jimmy pulled a face and shrugged. "I stopped at the end of the driveway up to the stables. Parnell was right next to the fence, so I got some really good photos, but I still can't be sure it's the same horse as in the Instagram photo. Did you find out anything, Chief?"

"Plum wasn't there but I don't think she's LP," he said as he noticed the wildlife book tucked under his sergeant's arm.

"You spotted anything else?" he asked, nodding towards the book. Since speaking to Ben, he'd been feeling more conciliatory towards his younger colleagues.

Jimmy's face brightened. "Yep, there was a heron over the duck pond and I think I've just seen two magpies?"

"Two for joy—that's meant to be lucky. If you only see one you should salute it, and say 'Good morning, Mr Magpie'," said Shadow.

"Why's that, Chief?" Shadow furrowed his brow. "Something to do with the Bible and warding off bad luck. I forget why exactly—my grandfather always did it." He nodded over the road to the dower house. "Let's go and see if Sybil is at home."

They walked across to the wisteria-clad house and Shadow raised the gleaming brass door knocker shaped like a lion's head and rapped twice on the door. After waiting a moment, he tried again.

"She won't be in, love," called out a now familiar voice behind them. The two detectives turned around to see Bet putting up the umbrellas at the picnic tables outside the pub. They walked back across the road to join her. "She'll be up at the castle. There's always an estate meeting on the second

Thursday of the month."

"Is this the same meeting that Lady Victoria is attending?"

"Yes, she's bound to be there too," agreed Bet, who had now started wiping down the tables.

"But not the duke?" queried Shadow who had checked and knew that the duke and his party were at the races again this afternoon. Bet shook her head with a smile.

"I can't say I blame him. He's got three horses running today. Watching them will be a lot more fun than being stuck on his office talking about which of those damp old tunnels to restore or which tenants are behind with the rent."

"I guess he's lucky his mother and sister don't mind attending on his behalf," said Jimmy. Bet arched a heavily pencilled eyebrow.

"I'd like to see anyone trying to stop those two attending," she replied curtly. "It was the same even when Bertie's dad, the old duke was alive. He'd be down at the stables with Flynn, while Sybil ran the estate. Last year's stroke might not have killed her but moving out of the castle when Annabel arrived almost did."

"I heard she's always been very involved in village life," said Shadow diplomatically.

"That's one way of putting it, I suppose. Nothing happens in Kirkdale without Her Grace knowing about it," replied Bet. From inside the pub a telephone started to ring. "I'll have to answer that. Are you two staying for a drink?"

she asked.

"No thank you," replied Shadow.

"I'll see you later then, Handsome," she called before disappearing through the door.

"Not a word," muttered Shadow to his grinning sergeant.

THEY DROVE BACK to the city, dropping down from the wild rolling moors into the low flat vale of York. In the distance, the Minster stood out against the horizon, towering over the city as it had done for hundreds of years.

"What are we going to do next, Chief?" asked Jimmy.

Shadow sighed. "The more I think about it, the more certain I am that Siobhan is responsible for Aidan's injuries, but we don't have anywhere near enough evidence to get a conviction. We really need to find a motive."

"Any ideas?"

"I'm sure there must a connection with the races. Ideally, I'd like to organise a surveillance operation at the course before the meeting ends on Saturday, but we'd need several officers to assist and the chief constable's permission."

"Do you think she'll give it?"

"I've got a meeting with her at five. I'll ask her then, but in betting terms I don't like my odds."

CHAPTER EIGHT

Across 4. Initially Fred, Ian and Xander alter the odds in their favour (3 letters)

"ABSOLUTELY NOT, SHADOW," said the chief constable firmly. "I don't have any officers to spare. Besides, you can't even tell me exactly what you are investigating. It sounds far more likely to me that Aidan O'Doyle had an argument with somebody outside the pub than this idea you have of someone riding cross-country to attack him."

Shadow attempted to protest, but she silenced him.

"I don't want you poking about at the racecourse upsetting people. Is that clear?" she said. "Surely I don't need to tell you how important the Ebor meeting is for the city? You've already ruffled enough feathers amongst the Duke of Kirkdale's party. You do know the dowager duchess used to be lady-in-waiting to the late queen mother, don't you? I don't want you upsetting any more VIPs. We even have members of the Saudi royal family arriving tomorrow, so stay away."

Shadow didn't bother trying to argue. He knew she wouldn't change her mind, so he turned and left her office with nothing more than a polite: "Yes ma'am."

THAT EVENING HE was due to have dinner at the Golden Dragon, the restaurant on Goodramgate that Jimmy's family owned. Since he and Jimmy started working together, he dined there once a week with his sergeant's family. When he arrived, he found Sophie and Jimmy sitting at the table next to the kitchen along with Jimmy's elderly grandfather. Shadow sat down and broke the bad news about the surveillance operation to Jimmy, but his sergeant didn't seem too disappointed.

"Then we'll have to go for plan B," he said, handing his boss a beer.

"What's plan B?" asked Shadow.

"Well," said Sophie leaning forward, "I didn't like your chances of getting the chief constable to agree to a surveillance operation, so I thought if she said no, then we could go to the races anyway. I'm not working on Saturday and you two must both have leave due. My parents have been members at York for years. They have four tickets for Saturday, so we can use them."

"You could ask Maggie to join us," suggested Jimmy. "Didn't you say she follows some of Flynn's horses? It would be good to have someone with us who knows a bit about racing."

"That's a great idea," agreed Sophie suspiciously quickly, "then if we do happen to bump into the chief constable or anyone else we know, they won't think we are up to anything. It'll look like a social outing rather than work. Do you want me to ask Maggie for you, Chief?"

Shadow shifted uncomfortably in his seat. He had the distinct feeling of being ambushed.

"No thank you, Sophie, it's fine. I'll ask her. I'll explain there's nothing in it and that we are only going there to help George out."

"If you put it like that, how could she resist?" replied Sophie, shaking her head. "That's one problem solved, but it doesn't help the fact that the three of us know nothing about betting. How will we even know if something dodgy is going on?"

"Ah ha," said Jimmy producing a copy of the *Racing Post* from the inside of his jacket, "I thought Grandad could have a look at the runners and riders for Saturday and give us his opinion. He's great at working out odds and things like that. When he was younger, he used to work in the casinos in Macau. I thought he could give us a crash course. I've circled all the FitzAllan horses, so he can see if there's anything strange."

Jimmy handed the newspaper over to his grandfather. The old man adjusted his spectacles as he peered at the list of runners and riders.

"Can he read English?" whispered Sophie.

"He's fine with numbers," Jimmy whispered back. The old man retrieved the stub of a pencil from behind his ear and began scribbling symbols on the page. Shadow watched him and could only assume they were Chinese numbers. Then he began talking rapidly to his grandson. Jimmy's forehead wrinkled as he listened, replied, and nodded before translating back to Shadow and Sophie.

"He says there's something strange about the third race. There are two FitzAllan horses running, Kirkdale Legend and Wantage Whisper, but he doesn't understand why Kirkdale Legend has been entered. I've explained that Siobhan told the Chief and I that he's got a good pedigree."

"I'm not sure that's the right word for a horse," interrupted Sophie. "I think they are thoroughbreds."

"Really? Okay, I might not have translated it right," said Jimmy looking confused, "but basically, Legend's parents won loads of races, but he's only won one. Grandad says he is completely outclassed by the other horse entered in his race."

At that moment, Rose—Jimmy's mother—appeared with their food and Jimmy's grandfather continued to try and explain the intricacies of betting and horse racing as they ate.

"Is Angela not joining us tonight?" asked Shadow quietly, after a particularly garbled explanation about how to calculate betting odds from Jimmy. He had a feeling Jimmy's sister would have been a better translator.

"She's gone to the Van Gogh immersive exhibition at St Mary's with Tom," replied Sophie. "You know the one where they project images on the walls, and you feel like you are actually in the painting? It's meant to be amazing. Have you been?"

Shadow shook his head. It was years since he'd been to a gallery or concert. Sophie turned around and began searching through her handbag that was slung over the back of her chair.

"Here, I picked up a couple of leaflets about it. Why don't you take one? You might enjoy it," she said, handing over the neatly folded piece of paper. Shadow briefly took in the vivid images before slipping it into his pocket.

"Thanks. Tom and Angela seem to be seeing a lot of each other," he commented.

"Yes, isn't it great?" said Sophie happily.

Shadow didn't reply, as he suspected Sophie and Jimmy had the enthusiasm shared by many happy couples of wanting to pair off all their friends and family too. The meal ended and thankfully so did the betting crash course.

"I'm still not sure if the bookies want a favourite to win or not." Jimmy sighed, scratching his head as he stared at the figures his grandfather had scribbled down.

"Never mind, sweetie," said Sophie with an affectionate smile, "you'll probably be able to work it out by Saturday."

LATER THAT NIGHT, after his obligatory game of backgammon with Jimmy's grandfather, Shadow arrived back on *Florence* and was noisily greeted by the geese who had taken up residence on his roof. Inside the boat the air was stale and stuffy, so he opened the windows to let a breeze blow through. He poured himself a glass of wine, removed his shoes and tie and opened the envelope Tom had left on his desk for him. Inside was a copy of the late duke's obituary from *The Times*, and some plans of Kirkdale Castle.

Shadow began reading the obituary. It mentioned Xander DeVere's education at Eton, his time at Sandhurst, then in the House of Lords and the many committees and associations he'd been a member of, but one sentence caught his eye: 'His army career ended abruptly after a tour of Northern Ireland, although he maintained close ties to the people he'd met there.' Shadow flicked through the papers, but there was no other mention of the late duke leaving the army.

He turned his attention to the plan of the castle. Tom had attached a note saying it was the most recent one he could find and that he'd downloaded it from the planning portal for North Yorkshire Council, when six months ago permission had been sought to replace some windows in the east wing. Shadow adjusted his glasses and peered at the small print on the plans. He noted with interest that despite being married for only a few months, the duke and duchess had separate bedrooms. The plan also showed two priest holes, one in the now disused chapel and one in the dining room. There were also two hidden passageways. One led from the main hallway down to the cellars and another from the library upstairs to the main landing. Shadow had a feeling he was looking at something important, but he wasn't sure why.

With a yawn, he finished his wine and went to bed, but sleep escaped him. The day's racegoers were still noisily celebrating, and their shouts and laughter echoed down from the many pubs that lined the river and in through his open windows. After an hour of tossing and turning, he stomped through to the sitting room and closed the windows with a bang so loud he woke up the geese who protested loudly from on the roof.

"For crying out loud," he muttered to himself as he flopped back into bed. As he thumped his pillow, he noticed the picture of Luisa smiling back at him. "I know, I know, I've turned into an old misery," he said closing his eyes while the geese continued their noisy tap dance above his head.

THE NEXT MORNING found Shadow frowning at his reflection in the tall mirror in front of him. Over his left shoulder he could see the shop assistant wearing an eager expression and a tape measure around his neck. Over his right shoulder stood Maggie with her arms folded and eyebrows raised.

"Stop scowling," she ordered. "You look very smart."

Shadow looked down at the navy blazer and chinos she had picked out for him. Then she and the assistant had completed his new look with a pale blue shirt and tie. *It could be worse*, he thought, and he couldn't recall the last time he'd been shopping for new clothes. This had been Maggie's only prerequisite before agreeing to go to the races with him when he'd called into the laundry and asked her, a little over an hour earlier.

"Okay, I'll come along, but only if you promise not to wear that old wax jacket. Honestly, one of these days it'll get up and walk out of here on its own."

Shadow hadn't protested, as she'd practically marched him down to the men's outfitters on Petergate, but he hadn't expected to be given a complete makeover either. He tried to view his reflection objectively. Perhaps it wasn't too bad. Just as he was beginning to get used to his new look, Maggie handed him a Panama hat.

"The finishing touch!" she declared.

"You must be joking?" Shadow replied, recoiling.

Maggie raised her eyebrows again. "Do you want to help George or not? This will make you blend in and it'll help to hide your face on the off-chance the chief constable is there too. Be grateful we're only going to the Ebor and not Royal Ascot otherwise you'd be in top hat and tails."

AFTER MAGGIE HAD completed her work, Shadow returned to the station laden down with bags full of his new clothes that he dumped in his office before anyone could see them. A few minutes later, Jimmy put his head around the door.

"Morning, Chief, I'm working on the photo of the horse. The guy from the Instagram account has been in touch. Do you need me for anything else?" he asked.

Shadow shook his head. "No but let me know if you find anything and get Tom to come and see me, will you?"

Five minutes later Tom appeared, and Shadow handed over a scribbled handwritten note.

"This is the name of the town FitzAllan and O'Doyle both came from and this is the date the late duke, Alexander DeVere, left the army. He was a captain at the time. Have a look and see if you can find anything strange that happened, any link to our case."

Tom returned an hour later and proudly laid out several sheets of paper in front of Shadow.

"I think I've found something sir," he said eagerly. "The town where FitzAllan and O'Doyle lived has its own weekly newspaper, so I started searching through archived copies from around the date you gave me. The only time the late duke, or Captain DeVere as he was called then, is mentioned is in a statement regarding the death of a young private in his unit. He says all the usual things—'outstanding service' and 'condolences to the family'—but reading between the lines it sounded as if his death was due to a lack of planning for the operation he was involved in."

"Whose fault would that be?" asked Shadow.

"The commanding officer's, in this case Captain DeVere, but that isn't the most interesting bit, sir. The name of the solider killed is Private FitzAllan," said Tom with a note of triumph as he pointed to the piece of the article he'd high-lighted.

Shadow looked up. "Flynn's father?"

"Yes, sir. If you read on a bit further, they mention Private FitzAllan left a young widow and baby son."

Shadow leaned back in his chair. Finally, they had found the connection between FitzAllan and the late duke. His thoughts drifted to another young widow and baby son connected to the DeVere family.

"Can I go now, sir?"

Shadow looked up a little startled. He had forgotten Tom was there for a moment.

"Yes, of course, Tom, off you go and well done."

The young constable left his office and Shadow returned to thinking about what this new information might mean for their current case and why nobody had mentioned it before.

AT AROUND MIDDAY, Shadow accepted Jimmy's offer to get him a sandwich for lunch. He really couldn't face fighting for a table in any of the crowded city pubs he usually frequented.

"Any progress with the photo of the horse?" he asked, as Jimmy placed the paper bag and cup of takeaway coffee on his desk. Shadow peered inside the bag and sniffed. "There isn't anything funny in here like mango or avocado is there?" He didn't trust the fashionable sandwich bars his sergeant was so fond of.

"No, Chief, just plain ham and cheese on white like you asked for," Jimmy reassured him. "Re the photo, the guy who posted it is called Callum. He and his brother Craig come down from Aberdeen every year for the races. It usually coincides with Craig's birthday, you see. This year it's his fortieth." Shadow made a winding motion with his hand as he took a large bite of sandwich and Jimmy hurried on. "Anyway their train was late getting in and they were on their way to their hotel in a taxi when they spotted the horse and took a snap. We managed to make the photo he took a bit clearer and I'm sure it's Parnell."

"But no sign of Siobhan at all? A hand, the back of her head?"

"No but we did manage to trace the taxi they were in and checked the driver's dash cam footage. He was driving along Tadcaster Road about three minutes before George's crash and as he passes the Lucky Horseshoe there's a quick flash of something that could be a horse's tail."

"Is it the right colour?"

"It's in black and white, Chief, but at least it proves there was something there," said Jimmy as upbeat as ever.

"All right thank you, Sergeant," replied Shadow trying not to sound disappointed. They might be making progress, but it was painfully slow and nowhere near enough to really help George yet.

Shadow spent the rest of the afternoon reading through the case notes, checking to see if any detail had been overlooked. Ben and Ollie had provided him with transcripts from both of FitzAllan's and O'Doyle's phones. All messages and call records on the burner he and Jimmy had found had been deleted. On FitzAllan's burner there were no photos and only prosaic texts like 'can't wait to see you' and 'last night was wonderful'. Apart from those of the burner phones, all other numbers were accounted for and none were located in either the Republic or Northern Ireland. Aidan's transcripts were even duller than Flynn's, so instead Shadow turned his attention to studying the horses who were due to run the next day.

The Minster bells were striking five o'clock by the time he was preparing to leave for the evening. He'd just reached for his jacket when there was a knock at the door.

"Yes," he called out. The door opened and Tom, Ben and Ollie trooped into his office, all looking unusually serious.

Shadow raised an eyebrow. "What's this? A deputation?"

The three young men glanced at each other nervously. Tom cleared his throat.

"We heard you and Jimmy were planning on going to the races tomorrow and we want to go too, sir."

Shadow sighed; Jimmy was incapable of keeping anything quiet.

"I think you may be overstating my importance, Constable. I have no control over how or where you choose to spend your free time."

"What Tom means is we want to go there and help with the investigation," said Ben.

Shadow pulled on his jacket as he surveyed his younger colleagues. "The chief constable has refused us permission to carry out any work related to the investigations during the race meeting," he replied.

"We know, but we've got a plan," announced Ollie. "Tom is going to be undercover…"

Shadow groaned and held up his hand in protest. "Stop right there. I don't need to hear any more," he said. The idea of Tom, Ben and Ollie involved in any sort of undercover work was the stuff of nightmares.

"Hold on, Chief," pleaded Ben. "Tom's going to be a waiter in the stand that has all the private boxes."

"My mum works there, so she can get me a job," added Tom.

"While he's working, Ben and I are going to wait somewhere inconspicuous, maybe the gents'," chimed in Ollie.

Shadow shook his head. This plan was sounding more ludicrous by the second. His forensics team and the word 'inconspicuous' simply did not fit together.

"Tom is going to bring items out of the duke's box, say a wine glass Lord Eastwold has held or the duke's knife. We can lift the prints off and then check them against the one on the mobile phone you found at the tunnel entrance."

"What would be the point?" asked Shadow in exasperation. "Even if this plan of yours worked, and I very much doubt it will, any evidence you find will be inadmissible."

"But at least it would help point us in the right direction. We've hit a brick wall with the phones and the thumbprint is all we have. If we find out who that belongs to, we might be able to discount some suspects," argued Ben as Shadow continued to shake his head.

Then Tom stepped forward. "Please, Chief," he begged, "we really want to help George. He's always been good to the three of us."

"He's patient and supportive and helpful. We owe him a lot," added Ben.

"He never minds if we ask a stupid question or if we muck something up," said Ollie.

Unlike me, thought Shadow. He studied their eager young faces for a moment, then sighed.

"All right, I'll agree to your mad idea, but on the strict understanding that you all keep a low profile. I want you to promise that the second anything goes wrong, if anyone involved in the case spots you, the three of you make yourselves scarce."

"Understood, Chief," replied Ollie with the other two nodding beside him.

"And for crying out loud be careful."

WITH A DEFINITE feeling of foreboding, he left the station and went to Catania's on Goodramgate. It was another of his favourite Italian restaurants and despite being full of racegoers, Gino, the owner still managed to find a table for him.

"This must be one of your busiest weeks," Shadow commented as yet another large party arrived.

Gino smiled broadly. "Isn't it wonderful! We are fully booked every evening when the races are on and this year it's been even better. We have been busy at lunchtimes too. Making up picnic hampers for people to take with them to the clock tower enclosure. They have been so popular."

"Very enterprising," agreed Shadow.

"All Carla's idea," said Gino proudly as he hurried back to the kitchen. Shadow watched him go and managed to catch a glimpse of Carla, Gino and Maria's daughter, carefully carrying a huge stack of plates. He shook his head. When he'd first started visiting Catania and La Scuola Femminile, Marco and Carla were only babies and now they were both grown-up and fully involved in their family businesses. That really did make him feel old.

After demolishing a huge plate of focaccia and lasagne,

Shadow returned to *Florence*, poured a glass of wine and considered the case. There were so many loose threads, it seemed impossible to bring them all together. Despite feeling sure Siobhan had attacked Aidan, he still didn't know why. The identity of LP was still a mystery, as was which Lumley gun had been used to kill Flynn. He would also like to know who had made sure the chief constable was aware of Sybil's connections to royalty.

When he finally laid his head on the pillow, he closed his eyes and hoped for a less disturbed night. Above him the geese's tap dance had turned into more of a soft shoe shuffle, which was at least a slight improvement. For the first time that week, he fell into a deep sleep. However, he didn't dream of the case but of his mother and grandparents. They were picnicking by the edge of the Kirkdale duck pond with Luisa. All of them were waving to him as he tried to row Maggie across in a little boat to meet them. It didn't matter how hard they tried though, they didn't get any closer. When he woke up the next morning, he felt strangely alone.

SHADOW HAD AGREED to meet the others at the Golden Dragon, so they could all take a taxi together to the Knavesmire. The first thing he noticed was that Jimmy had been given a makeover too. His sergeant was dressed in a cream linen suit and a gleaming pair of dark brown brogues.

It was the first time Shadow had seen his feet encased in anything other than expensive trainers. The aviator-style sunglasses on his face couldn't detract from the huge grin on his face when he saw his boss.

"Hey get you, Chief! You look great!" he enthused. Shadow grunted.

"It's all Maggie's doing. Hello, Sophie, you look very nice," he said politely turning to the pathologist. In truth, he almost hadn't recognised her. Usually he saw her wearing scrubs, with her hair scraped back and her face free of make-up. Today however, she had changed into a simple black shift dress and heels with a pale pink pashmina draped over her shoulders. Her make-up was still minimal but her long blonde hair was hanging loose and on her head was a huge black hat trimmed with feathers around the brim.

"Thanks, Chief," Sophie replied with a smile. "You don't scrub up too bad yourself."

At that moment, the taxi arrived, and Maggie came hurrying out of the laundry, slightly out of breath. She was wearing a navy lace dress with cream shoes and she carried a matching bag. There was a cream saucer-shaped fascinator perched on the side of her head, holding her dark curls in place.

"Sorry I'm late," she gasped. "I needed the girls to give me a hand with my hat."

"You look lovely," said Shadow holding the car door open for her.

"Worth ditching the wax jacket for?" she asked with a grin.

"Definitely," he replied.

As the taxi inched along Tadcaster Road behind the rest of the traffic going to the races, Shadow's nose began to twitch. The feathers on Sophie's hat kept making him want to sneeze as she dished out their badges for the county stand. Maggie and Sophie tied the blue and gold discs on to their handbags, while Shadow attached his to the button of his blazer. Jimmy had brought his bird-spotting binoculars with him and was attempting to tie his ticket on to the strap around his neck.

"I've seen all the racegoers do this. Some of them must have about twenty tied on," he said, twisting his head to one side at an awkward angle so he could see what he was doing.

"Let me help before you strangle yourself," tutted Sophie with an indulgent smile as she took over and swiftly attached the badge to the strap. A few minutes later and they had barely moved.

"It might be quicker to walk," suggested Maggie. The others all nodded in agreement, so Shadow paid the driver and they stepped out on to Tadcaster Road and joined the crowds heading to the Knavesmire.

It was an hour before the first race, but the place was already heaving. There was a heady mix of serious gamblers, racing enthusiasts and people simply there for a good time. Young women in elaborate outfits posed for photographers outside the grandstand. Families picnicked in the alcohol-free clocktower enclosure. Helicopters circled overhead before depositing wealthy foreign owners, corporate sponsors and famous international jockeys at the edge of the course. Two large black Range Rovers glided through the crowd and pulled up to the door of the county stand that contained the private boxes and the restaurants and bars for the members and owners and trainers.

Jimmy and Shadow watched as the Duke of Kirkdale and his party stepped out. The photographers swarmed round as soon as they spotted Annabel DeVere, today wearing a cream silk dress that reached almost to her ankles and a deep-brimmed pink hat. Ignoring the snapping cameras, she swept along in vertiginous cream heels. The duke, Lord and Lady Eastwold, Sir Charles and Sybil followed her through the main doors being held open by uniformed security guards.

"Well, it looks like they're all here," said Jimmy as his phone began to beep. He checked the screen. "It's Tom. He said he's managed to get a job waiting in the duke's box and Ben and Ollie are hiding in a store cupboard on the same corridor."

Shadow shook his head and sighed heavily.

"Does Tom even know how to do silver service?" he asked.

"Yes, he used to do it as a holiday job when he was a student," said Sophie.

"He helped me and Angela out at the restaurant when

Mum was ill a couple of months ago," added Jimmy. "He'll be fine."

"I hope so for all our sakes," muttered Shadow.

They began to stroll around and found their way to the parade ring where the horses for the first race were being led around by their stable lads and lasses.

In the centre of the parade ring, jockeys wearing brightly coloured silks chatted to owners or were given final instructions by the trainers, before mounting their horses. Then one by one they left the parade ring and cantered down to the starting stalls. Shadow spotted Siobhan with the jockey who was due to ride her horse. Judging by the amount of hand gestures and finger pointing she had very clear ideas of what he should be doing when he got in the saddle. He was wearing purple and gold silks.

"Aren't those the Duke of Kirkdale's colours?" asked Shadow.

Jimmy consulted his race card. "Yes, the horse is Diamond Dealer," he replied. "What colours would you choose if you owned a racehorse?"

"I guess I'd be patriotic and go for red, white and blue," replied Sophie.

Maggie shook her head. "From a purely professional point of view, I'd pick brown, but even then, they must be hell to keep clean."

When the last of the horses had left, they moved away from the parade ring and went to view the race from the steps of the grandstand. Amidst much cheering and shouting they watched as Diamond Dealer romped home in first place.

"That's a good start for the duke," commented Jimmy.

"Let's get a drink to celebrate on his behalf," suggested Shadow, struggling to make himself heard above the noise.

Several huge marquees had been erected to cater for the crowds that couldn't all be accommodated in the grandstand. Jimmy managed to locate a table in the champagne and oyster tent, while Shadow fought his way to the bar and returned with a bottle of fizz, three glasses and a mineral water for Jimmy.

"Cheers," said Maggie, raising her glass, "here's to a successful day."

"Cheers," the others echoed. Sophie raised her eyebrows at Jimmy, and he cleared his throat.

"I thought Sophie and I might go and see if we can find Siobhan anywhere. Why don't you two stay here and hold the table. If we lose it, I bet we won't get another one."

"Hey, your first bet of the day!" Sophie grinned.

Jimmy's face lit up. "You're right. I don't even know what I'm saying sometimes."

"Sometimes?" grunted Shadow half to himself.

"Oh, to be young and in love," Maggie laughed as Sophie and Jimmy left the tent arm in arm. She turned to Shadow. "How's George doing? He must be worried?"

Shadow nodded. "He is, but he's trying to keep himself

busy. I'm sure the stress of it all is getting to him, but at least he has Carol to look after him."

"Yes, he's lucky not to be on his own like you and me at a time like this."

"Don't you enjoy living alone?" he asked. Maggie had been divorced for over ten years and her only son now lived in Spain.

"I wouldn't say I enjoy it, but I've got used to it. I miss Sam of course since he moved out and it would be nice to have someone to get rid of the odd spider in the bath."

"I didn't know you were scared of spiders."

"Oh, I can't stand the horrid creatures, scurrying around and lurking in corners," Maggie replied with a shudder. Shadow chuckled and she arched an eyebrow at him. "Oh, I suppose a chief inspector isn't afraid of anything."

"That's where you are wrong. I suffer from severe novinophobia."

"What's that?"

"Fear of running out of wine," said Shadow with a smile as he reached over and topped Maggie's glass up.

She threw her head back and laughed her deep, throaty laugh. "You know when you aren't being grumpy, you can be very good company."

"Well, that's where you have the advantage, Maggie. Even when you are at your most bossy, you are still charming."

Maggie flushed with pleasure, but before she could respond a familiar voice from the other side of the bar shouted across.

"Well, hello again, Handsome!"

Shadow looked up to see a very merry Bet blowing him a kiss.

"A friend of yours?" asked Maggie coolly.

"She's the barmaid from the pub in Kirkdale, the village where Flynn FitzAllan lived. Apparently, she has a thing for coppers."

"Well, aren't you the lucky one!"

"There's no accounting for taste." Shadow shrugged. "And speaking of people I would rather avoid…" He nodded towards a chubby, bearded figure standing a few metres away. Bob was one of the city window cleaners, who was a keen gambler and had clearly already spent plenty of time and money in the bar.

"Uh-oh, he's heading our way. Let's make a move," Maggie whispered, but they were too late.

"Hello there, you two," Bob said loudly as he walked a little unsteadily towards them. "Fancy seeing you here. Had any winners?"

"Not placed a bet yet. How about you, Bob?" replied Shadow.

"Oh, I've been here every day this week. I'm about breaking even at the minute," he said, which Shadow mentally translated as meaning he'd lost a packet. "But I've got high hopes for the third race. I've just stuck two hundred quid on Kirkdale Legend."

"Two hundred!" exclaimed Maggie. Shadow consulted the odds up on the television screens in the bar.

"It's a hundred-to-one shot," he said in disbelief.

"If it comes in, I'm taking the wife on a cruise to the Caribbean."

"If it doesn't, I wouldn't bother going home," said Maggie under her breath. Bob, swaying slightly, leaned forward and beckoned the two of them to listen closely.

"I reckon it's a cert," he whispered. "I was behind that Lord Eastwold in the queue for one of the course bookies. He put a grand on it to win. I asked around and he'd done the same with a few of the other bookies. So, I thought if it's good enough for a toff like him, it's good enough for me. I heard his brother-in-law owns the horse. The posh lot always stick together. Why don't you put a couple of quid on too before the price goes down? I'll see you later. I've got a pint with my name on it."

He staggered off, leaving Shadow frowning and Maggie rummaging for her purse in her handbag.

"What are you doing?" Shadow asked.

"Going to put a bet on."

"You're not seriously taking a tip from Bob, are you? If he really knew what he was doing, do you think he'd still be cleaning windows?"

"Oh, come on where's your sense of adventure? It's fun to have the odd flutter," she teased. "Who knows maybe I'll end up in the Caribbean too."

She tottered off to the nearest bookie, leaving Shadow behind still frowning. Siobhan had called Kirkdale Legend a liability and even Jimmy's grandfather had questioned why he was running in such a prestigious race. Had Eastwold heard some inside information or was he so desperate financially that he needed a big win on an outsider? Was he that reckless? What had he said as Shadow had helped him out of the restaurant? "All his problems would be solved after the weekend, in a heartbeat." Shadow glanced down at the race card. The name of the next race was the Heart of Yorkshire Cup. At that moment, Jimmy and Sophie reappeared.

"You on your own, Chief?" asked Jimmy.

Shadow nodded, still a little distracted. "Against my advice, Maggie has gone to place a bet on a hundred-to-one outsider in the next race."

"What made her do that?" asked Sophie.

"A tip from Bob, would you believe," sighed Shadow and briefly recounted the conversation he'd had with the window cleaner. No sooner had he finished than Sophie was heading out of the bar too.

"Not you as well?" said Shadow in exasperation.

"Are you sure, Soph?" asked Jimmy a little nervously.

Sophie turned back, grinning at the two detectives.

"At a hundred to one it's got to be worth a fiver," she said with a shrug.

"How much do you think Eastwold has put on in total?" asked Jimmy.

"I don't know, but he's not going to be very popular with the bookies if Kirkdale Legend does win," replied Shadow.

"Who's the favourite?"

Shadow turned and squinted at the screen again.

"Wantage Whisper. The other FitzAllan horse. He's at two to one with the odds shortening."

Jimmy fixed his eyes on the screen too.

"Look, Chief, Kirkdale Legend's dropped to ninety to one now."

"I'm not surprised. God only knows how many people Bob and Maggie have spoken to by now," replied Shadow, shaking his head.

CHAPTER NINE

Down 7. Snug is the last thing you feel when they go bang! (4 letters)

A FEW MINUTES later, Maggie and Sophie returned looking very pleased with themselves.

"Come on let's go and see the horses before they go down to the stalls," said Sophie.

"Shall we?" asked Shadow offering Maggie his arm. The four of them left the bar and made their way through the crowds. They sauntered over to the paddock where the horses were beginning to parade. Jimmy consulted his race card as two black horses went by, flaring their nostrils and tossing their manes. One had a white mark on his nose, but both jockeys were wearing the purple and gold silks of the Duke of Kirkdale.

"Hey look, there are the two horses from the FitzAllan stable: Kirkdale Legend and Wantage Whisper."

"Which one is which?" asked Sophie.

"Kirkdale Legend is the one without the white mark on his nose," replied Jimmy.

"He's magnificent. Definitely looks like a winner to me,"

said Sophie confidently as, the horses passed by once again.

"According to his trainer, he's a liability," replied Shadow, who was still trying to work out why Eastwold would place such a large sum on the horse.

"If he was mine, I think I'd call him Lloyd," said Jimmy.

"Just Lloyd?" queried Shadow, thinking such a simple name was uncharacteristically understated for his sergeant.

"Yep, like the bank. You know it's got the black horse for a symbol. I love their adverts. That one when the horse is with the soldier in the First World War, then he's delivering milk to the little girl and at the end he's running along the beach."

"Oh, I love that one too," agreed Maggie. "I don't know why, but it always makes me cry."

"I read somewhere they had to use five horses to film all the sequences," said Sophie.

"How did they find five that looked exactly the same?" asked Jimmy.

"I guess to most people a black horse is, just a black horse," she said taking another sip of her champagne.

"We're having a similar problem with a chestnut horse," sighed Jimmy, as the last horse left the parade ring. The party of four made their way to the steps in front of the grandstand. The horses were all in their stalls, under starters orders, and suddenly they were off. The crowd roared their approval, but while everyone's attention was focused on the race, Shadow turned to look at the stand behind him. He had borrowed Jimmy's binoculars, raised them to his eyes and focused on the box belonging to the Duke of Kirkdale. His Grace and all his guests were out on the balcony. There was Sir Charles, Lord and Lady Eastwold, Annabel and Sybil, and Siobhan FitzAllan had joined them. Almost all of them looked animated as they shouted and cheered on their horses. Only Annabel turned away and Siobhan stood silently with her jaw tensed as she followed the race through her own binoculars.

Shadow replayed what Sophie had said in his head and lowered his binoculars. The crowd around him suddenly went wild. Sophie and Maggie were both screaming their heads off. Kirkdale Legend had done it. He'd won. Shadow glance back up at the box. The duke and Eastwood were spraying each other with champagne. Siobhan was staring out across the course. She didn't look remotely surprised by the result. By now Maggie and Sophie were jumping up and down and hugging each other.

"Congratulations," said Shadow. "Are you two going to collect your winnings or come to the winner's enclosure and see the duke receive the cup?"

"I think we should go and cash in before Lord Eastwold gets there," said Maggie. "He might clean them out."

"Then we'll see you back in the champagne tent," said Shadow as he motioned for Jimmy to follow him.

"Not the result the bookies were expecting, Chief," commented Jimmy as they pushed their way through the crowds.

"Not the result anyone was expecting except Siobhan by the look of things," muttered Shadow. "What's wrong with you?" he asked impatiently as Jimmy limped along by his side.

"It's these new shoes, Chief. They're killing my feet," Jimmy replied with a grimace as he glanced down at his shiny brogues. "I'm only really used to wearing trainers, but Soph insisted on proper shoes today. She said it would be good practice for the wedding."

Down at the winners' enclosure there was much cheering as Kirkdale Legend arrived, covered in sweat and with nostrils flaring. Siobhan was there to greet the horse and jockey, and a few seconds later the duke arrived grinning wildly. Looking even more pleased with herself was Lavinia trotting along behind him, but there was no sign of either of their spouses. The duke shook Siobhan and the jockey by the hand before striding over to the be presented with the Heart of Yorkshire Cup by the Lady Mayoress of York. Then they all posed next to the horse before he was led away. A loud whooping sound to his left caught Shadow's attention. It was Bet, cheering for all she was worth as the duke lifted his trophy for another photograph.

"She must have had a bet on Kirkdale Legend too," whispered Jimmy.

Shadow nodded, but his mind was elsewhere as he watched the black horse leave the enclosure.

"While everyone is distracted by the next race, let's go and have a look at the stables," he whispered. The two detectives slipped away and made their way back towards the parade ring and on to the saddling enclosure. Behind the enclosure was the weighing-in room and the stables. It was a hive of activity as everyone prepared for the next race. Trainers were shouting instructions, grooms were saddling up horses and jockeys were lining up to get weighed in.

"Where are we going, Chief?" whispered Jimmy.

"I want to have a closer look at the FitzAllan horses. Something isn't right, and I want to find out what's going on," Shadow replied. "Now follow me and try and look like you belong." Shadow strode purposefully through the stables with Jimmy, attempting to look nonchalant and whistling, close behind him. They stopped suddenly when they spotted the young stable lad Siobhan had berated back in at her yard in Kirkdale. He and another groom were checking the bridle on a chestnut filly, who kept rearing up. Neither of them noticed as Shadow and Jimmy edged past and around the corner to the next stalls. Inside were two black horses, covered in blankets with the FitzAllan logo and still sweating from their race.

"We've found them," whispered Shadow. "You go and see if there's anything strange about either of them."

Reluctantly Jimmy snuck into the first stall. The inhabitant turned his head and snorted loudly at him.

"Shush now, good horsey," said Jimmy softly. "He's got

a white mark Chief, so it's Wantage Whisper."

A roar from outside told them the next race had begun.

"Hurry up," hissed Shadow. "And try not to get kicked or bitten."

"I'm not really sure what I'm looking for, Chief," he replied.

I should have brought Sophie instead, thought Shadow impatiently as yet again Jimmy ducked out of the way of the horse who was inquisitively trying to nudge him with his nose.

"Let me try. You stand watch."

With a look of obvious relief, Jimmy stepped out of the stall and Shadow took his place.

"There now, steady lad," Shadow said quietly and gently laid his hand on the horse's left flank. Very slowly he reached forward with his other hand and delicately stroked Wantage Whisper between his eyes and along the length of his nose. Then just as slowly, he raised his palm. It was covered in a white creamy substance and the small white mark on the horse's nose was now smudged.

"What is it?" asked Jimmy. Shadow gingerly raised his hand to his nose and sniffed.

"I'm not sure, I don't recognise the smell," he said offering his hand to his sergeant. Jimmy leant forward and sniffed too.

"I do," he said with a smile. "It's the stuff you use to whiten old trainers."

Shadow shook his head in disbelief. "How on earth did they expect to get away with it? If a vet had carried out an examination, he would have spotted it straight away." At that moment, the horse pawed the ground with his front hoof sending bits of loose straw flying towards Shadow. He took this as his cue to leave and slowly edged back out of the stall.

"You stay here," Shadow ordered. "I'll go and find the clerk of the course. Do not let those two horses out of your sight and try not to upset them."

Shadow hurried out of the stables and through the crowds to the county stand, where the private boxes and offices for the course officials were situated. A burly security guard blocked his way.

"I'm sorry, sir, this entrance is only for those in a private box."

"I need to see the clerk of the course. It's urgent," said Shadow, putting his hand inside his pocket for his warrant card only to remember he'd left it in his old wax jacket.

"I'm sorry, sir, I can't let you through," repeated the guard firmly, but politely. Then over his shoulder Shadow spotted Sir Charles Richmond striding along the corridor. He did not look a happy man.

"Sir Charles!" Shadow called out. He remembered the MP was also on the board of the racecourse. The politician stopped when he heard his name and held up his hand in recognition when he saw Shadow.

"Let him through, let him through," he ordered, and the

six-foot-three security guard meekly stepped aside. Shadow hurried past.

"Sorry to interrupt you, Sir Charles," he began politely, but the MP shook his head.

"No need to apologise, I'm having a shocking day anyway. Just lost a packet on Wantage Whisper. Bertie and Eastwold backed Kirkdale Legend, but I thought they were crazy when I saw the odds. Why are you here? Is this about FitzAllan and his stable lad?"

"Yes, I think I've found a connection between their deaths and the bet you have just lost. I have reason to believe that two horses from the FitzAllan stable have been switched with each other," Shadow explained. The MP's mouth opened in astonishment as Shadow continued, "I have left my sergeant in the stables, but I need to see the clerk of the course."

Sir Charles immediately turned to the security guard. "Radio the clerk of the course and tell her to meet me at the stables and send two of your colleagues too," he ordered before turning back to Shadow. "Lead the way, Chief Inspector."

Shadow headed back towards the stables closely followed by Sir Charles. The clerk of the course, a smartly dressed woman in her mid-thirties, and two burly security guards were waiting for them at the entrance. Jimmy was still standing next to the two snorting and sweating horses and looked relieved to see them all.

"One of Siobhan's grooms asked me what I was doing here," he said. "I told him I was one of the course vets, but I don't think he believed me."

"What's going on, Shadow?" asked Sir Charles.

"The identities of these two horses have been switched. Wantage Whisper has had his white blaze hidden and Kirkdale Legend has been given one instead," Shadow explained.

Sir Charles stared at him incredulously.

"So Wantage Whisper, the favourite, actually won?" he asked.

"Yes," confirmed Shadow, as the clerk of the course opened the door of the nearest stall and calmly approached the horse inside. She began gently stroking his nose, while making reassuring noises, then lifted up the palm of her hand and showed it to Sir Charles. It was covered in a black powdery substance.

"I did the same to the other one," explained Shadow showing his own palm covered in white.

"What the hell do you think you are doing?"

They all turned around. Siobhan was standing behind them with her hands on her hips and a look of blind fury on her face.

"I could ask you the same, Siobhan," replied Sir Charles coolly.

"Get away from my horses," Siobhan demanded, pointing at the clerk of the course who had now turned her attention to the other horse. Shadow stepped forward.

"Siobhan FitzAllan, I am arresting you for…"

"The hell you are," she snarled, then before anyone could stop her, she pushed over a stack of straw bales, knocking both Shadow and Sir Charles off their feet as she fled towards the entrance.

"Get after her!" yelled Shadow from the stable floor. Jimmy and the two security guards leapt over the straw and chased her out of the door, while Shadow got to his feet and helped Sir Charles up.

"Are you all right?" he asked.

"Fine," replied the MP. "You go after them. I'll sort things out here with the course authorities."

Shadow hurried after Jimmy and the security guards. As soon as he was outside, he paused and looked around, but he couldn't see them anywhere, then he turned and spotted several figures running through the car park. He dashed after them and arrived out of breath, but just in time to see Jimmy catch up with Siobhan as she tried to climb into her horse-box.

"It's okay, Chief," his sergeant shouted. "We've got her, and I've called for backup. A car should be here soon."

"Then I'll go and see what the duke and Eastwold have to say about all this," replied Shadow. Jimmy gave him a thumbs up, then began to read Siobhan her rights as she continued to struggle and swear at the security guards who were helping to detain her.

At a slightly more sedate pace, Shadow headed back to the main area of the course. He noticed several worried-looking men wearing official badges heading to the stables as an announcement was broadcast over the tannoy system, declaring there was to be a stewards' inquiry into the result of the last race. This caused uproar amongst the punters who had torn up what they thought was a losing ticket and the bookies who had already begun paying out.

This time when the security guard saw Shadow, he stepped aside without being asked. Shadow climbed up three flights of stairs to the top floor where the private boxes were situated. The first person he saw was Tom, dressed in a pristine white waiter's uniform and balancing a stack of empty plates and glasses on a large tray.

"What's going on, sir? The duke and Lord Eastwold weren't very happy when they heard there's a stewards' inquiry. I don't think they've collected all their winnings yet. Eastwold dashed off in a real state," whispered Tom nodding towards the nearest door bearing the name Kirkdale.

"I'll go and see what they have to say?" said Shadow.

"Probably not much, sir. They have a guest up from London for the day. It's the family's solicitor. He must have been invited at the last minute because he isn't on the guest list."

"Just my luck," muttered Shadow. "By the way what's happening with—" he managed to stop himself saying Laurel and Hardy "—Ben and Ollie?"

"No luck so far, but a few minutes ago, I dropped off another glass for them to check for prints. They are in the storeroom opposite the gents' at the far end of the corridor. They've locked themselves in. If you want to speak to them, knock three times."

At that moment, the door into the kitchen opened and two waitresses came bustling out carrying champagne buckets full of ice. Shadow promptly stepped away from Tom, who nodded a quick goodbye before disappearing through the kitchen door. Then Shadow walked across the thickly carpeted corridor and knocked on the door belonging to the Duke of Kirkdale's private box. It was opened almost immediately by a young waitress and Shadow stepped inside.

It was arranged as an elegant private dining room with a television screen showing the races and betting information, and large sliding glass doors that opened on to a balcony with a perfect view of the winning post. Annabel was stand-ing on the balcony with her back to the room, Bertie was drinking champagne as he squinted at the screen and Lavinia was tucking into a large chocolate eclair. Huddled together in the corner, looking unusually concerned, was Sybil and a man Shadow didn't recognise. They stopped talking when they saw him. The dowager duchess was wearing a pretty lavender lace dress with matching hat and gloves.

"Hello there, Chief Inspector," she said, switching on her usual smile. "We wondered if we would be seeing you. Sir Charles just telephoned Bertie to let him know Siobhan has been placed under arrest. It's taken us all rather by surprise. I think you know everyone, except for our guest up from London. May I introduce Jolyon Dalrymple."

Shadow stepped forward and shook hands with the visitor.

"I say what's going on, Shadow?" asked the duke, jabbing his finger towards him. "I hear you've arrested my trainer."

"That's correct. Mrs FitzAllan has been taken into custody," replied Shadow, nodding politely to Annabel, who had now turned around and was standing in the balcony doorway.

"Well, that's no good. I have horses down to run in the next three races. You'll have to release her."

"Actually, I wanted to talk to you about your two horses that ran in the last race: Kirkdale Legend and Wantage Whisper," said Shadow.

"Who the hell ordered a stewards' inquiry anyway?" demanded the duke, ignoring the question.

"That would be the course stewards," explained Shadow patiently as Jolyon stepped forward and handed Shadow a business card.

"My client has nothing to say on the matter, but we shall be issuing a statement on His Grace's behalf in due course," he said smoothly. Shadow read the card. *Jolyon Dalrymple, Managing Partner, Dalrymple, Wiley and Jones, Fetter Lane, London.* Unfortunately, Tom had been correct.

"Thank you. I'll look forward to that," he replied slipping the card into his pocket, before turning to go. There was no point staying. With a top London lawyer present nobody would say anything of use to him.

"Why have you arrested her? Is it only to do with the horses?"

Shadow looked back in surprise. It was Annabel who had spoken.

"Your Grace, please allow me to handle this on your behalf," said the solicitor quietly, but Annabel had her eyes fixed on Shadow.

"Mrs FitzAllan has been arrested on suspicion of fraud and attempted murder," he replied. Annabel's expression didn't change; she merely nodded and stepped back out on to the balcony.

Shadow left the box and plodded down the corridor, wondering if it was merely bad luck on his part that the lawyer should be the duke's guest today, or had the family known what Siobhan was going to do with the horses and decided it would be useful to have the best legal advice close at hand? Tom had said it was a last-minute invitation. He arrived at the storeroom door and knocked three times. The door opened a couple of inches to reveal Ollie's face peering nervously through the gap, which then broke into a grin.

"Chief, I almost didn't recognise you. Where's the wax jacket?"

Shadow ignored the question. "Why are you wearing your protective suits? I thought you were meant to be undercover?" he asked as he stepped into the storeroom that his two colleagues had managed to turn into a mini lab.

"We thought they might be a good disguise. If anyone asks what we were doing, we are going to say we're pest control, investigating reports of cockroaches. Nobody likes cockroaches so they won't want to hang around," explained Ollie, clearly pleased with their ingenuity.

"I see, so have you managed to find a match?" asked Shadow without much hope.

"Yes, Chief, just now a perfect match to the thumbprint we found on the phone," replied Ben triumphantly, from his position crouched on the floor next to a laptop, several brushes, a jar of aluminium powder and various items of dirty crockery and cutlery.

"And?"

"It was on the last wine glass Tom brought us," added Ben.

"And?"

"It's Annabel, the duchess, Chief."

Shadow was silent for a moment. He was genuinely stunned that this hare-brained scheme had produced a result.

"Are you sure?"

"Yes, it's definitely her glass. Tom said she is the only one there drinking mineral water and there was only one set of prints on the glass."

"We've found something else weird too," said Ollie, "Tom brought us a glass Siobhan was drinking from, and on the prints we lifted there were traces of a white substance, but we haven't been able to identify it yet."

"I think you'll find it's the stuff you use to make trainers white again."

"You mean trainers as in running shoes, Chief?"

"Yes, it's a long story, but she used it change the appearance of a horse. Jimmy has just arrested her for the attempted murder of O'Doyle."

"Does that mean George is in the clear?" asked Ben eagerly, but Shadow held up his hand.

"Let's not get ahead of ourselves. Now make yourselves scarce before someone sees you. Oh, and well done."

With that, he left the scientists packing up their things and returned to the course, pushing his way through the crowds in search of a police car to take him back to the station.

WHEN HE ARRIVED back at the old guildhall, he found the custody suite was also full of racegoers, although most of these young men with their beer-stained suits and bloodied noses were now under arrest for affray and being drunk and disorderly.

"Has Mrs FitzAllan said anything yet?" Shadow asked the custody sergeant, who shook his head.

"No, Chief, not unless you count calling me every name

under the sun when I took her phones off her. We've already checked, and one of them is the one O'Doyle contacted before he died. Her brief's on her way, but she's been held up in all the race traffic. There is a young lady and gentleman waiting for you in the meeting room though, Chief."

"Who are they?" asked Shadow in surprise.

"They wouldn't give a name. They both seemed pretty nervous, especially when they heard Siobhan kicking off," replied the custody sergeant.

When Shadow opened the door of the meeting room, he found a frightened-looking Clancy and Giles huddled together on the sofa holding hands.

"I understand you wanted to see me," he said.

"I've come to confess," Clancy blurted out before he'd even sat down.

"Confess to what?" he asked.

Clancy took a deep breath, then her words came tumbling out in a rush. "I lied to you. When you asked me about Flynn and the wine stain on his shirt, I lied. I know I shouldn't have done. I repeated the story Flynn told me to tell anyone who asked. I suppose I panicked, and I still wanted to be loyal to Flynn. Do what he would want, but I know I was wrong and I'm really sorry."

Shadow held up his hand. The poor girl was close to tears.

"Please calm down. The main thing is you're here now. Would you like a glass of water before you continue?"

Clancy shook her head.

"No thank you."

"Then let's start at the beginning. Where was Flynn when his shirt got covered in wine?"

"At our cottage."

Giles groaned and put his head in his hands.

"Giles doesn't know anything about this, Chief Inspector," Clancy added quickly and giving her boyfriend an anxious look. "He was out in York celebrating Fred's twenty-first that night. I only told him this morning. I've been so worried. I knew you'd find out I'd lied eventually."

"If the DeVeres find out they could kick us out of the cottage and I could lose my job," said Giles.

Shadow was starting to feel confused. "Why was Flynn at your cottage?"

"He was meeting Annabel. They usually met at a cottage on Sir Charles Richmond's estate, but Annabel had told Flynn she needed to speak to him urgently and there was nowhere else for them to go. The yard was full of people and there was a ball or party or something going on at the castle. I knew Flynn wouldn't have asked me unless he was desperate."

Shadow stared at the young woman. Thanks to her and the thumbprint on the phone, suddenly it felt like things were falling into place.

"Did Flynn ever call Annabel LP as a nickname or something?"

"LP?" Clancy frowned for a second, before the answer came to her: "Oh, no that's what Siobhan calls her. She's always coming up with nicknames for people. It stands for Lady Penelope, you know from the old *Thunderbirds* TV show. Siobhan doesn't like Annabel much."

"Because she was having an affair with Flynn?" asked Shadow remembering from his childhood the jerky blonde puppet dressed in a pink suit she was referring to.

"No, Siobhan just generally doesn't like many people. It wasn't because she was jealous. Like I told you at the yard, Siobhan and Flynn's marriage has always been more of a business arrangement than a romance. Siobhan found out about the affair a few days before Flynn died, but she didn't care."

"What was Annabel wearing when she met Flynn at your cottage?" Shadow asked. What Clancy was telling him sounded believable, but he needed to be sure.

"This beautiful long white evening dress," replied Clancy immediately.

"What about the wine? I thought she didn't drink?"

"She wasn't that night, but she sometimes did when she was with Flynn. He brought a bottle of her favourite red with him to the cottage," said Clancy with a smile. "Honestly, Chief Inspector, if you could have seen them together. She was like a different person with him. Relaxed, smiling all the time. I dropped him off at the cottage to meet her once and she came running out, laughing she was so pleased to see him."

"But on that night in your cottage they argued, and she threw her glass of wine at him?"

"No, that's the thing." Clancy's voice caught in her throat and Giles placed his hand on hers. "They weren't arguing they were celebrating. Annabel was pregnant. When she told him, Flynn jumped up and threw his arms around her, he was still holding his glass of wine and they both got soaked, but they were so happy they didn't care." Clancy's lip was trembling, and her eyes were brimming with tears at the memory. Shadow passed her a box of tissues that were on the table and gave a wry smile.

"I take it that's how the carpet was stained too?"

Clancy nodded as recognition dawned on Giles's face.

"The white wine and salt didn't work by the way," he replied with a slight smile as he put his arm protectively around Clancy's shoulder. "Is she in a lot of trouble?"

"Is there anything else you haven't told me?" asked Shadow.

Clancy shook her head firmly. "No, I swear that's everything."

"Then I don't think we need to take this any further."

AFTER SHADOW HAD reassured Clancy and Giles several times that there was no need for them to worry, and that they were both free to return home, he made his way up to his office pondering what Clancy had told him. He found Jimmy waiting for him outside his door, his left hand now wrapped in a bandage.

"What happened to you?" he asked.

"I got bitten, Chief," explained Jimmy, raising his hand. "Sophie took me to the hospital for a tetanus shot."

"For crying out loud," Shadow muttered impatiently, "I told you to be careful around those horses."

"It wasn't a horse, Chief. It was Siobhan. She bit me after I'd arrested her and was trying to get her into the police car."

"Oh, then you did the right thing. Human bites can be nasty," replied Shadow, patting his sergeant on the shoulder, "and if all else fails we can charge her with assault."

"Speaking of nasty, the chief constable is on the warpath. She's arrived downstairs. Somebody told her we were at the races and she isn't very happy about it," said Jimmy, in what Shadow thought might rank as the understatement of the year. As his sergeant followed him into this office, Shadow noticed his limp was even more pronounced.

"It looks like you picked the wrong day stop wearing trainers."

"Tell me about it, Chief, my feet are covered in blisters." Jimmy winced as he eased off his left shoe. "I hope they don't hurt this much for the wedding." Shadow wrinkled his nose as the other shoe came off, worried that the socks would be next.

"Why don't you get yourself home. It's been a long day and I doubt we're going to get anything out of Siobhan this evening."

"Okay, Chief. If you're sure. Call if you need me."

With that he slowly limped out through the door, his shoes in hand and wearing only his socks. When he'd gone, Shadow picked up the phone. He needed to apologise to Maggie for leaving her at the course so abruptly. He dialled her mobile number and waited. It rang for an awfully long time before she finally answered. She stopped him as soon as he began to tell her how sorry he was.

"It's absolutely fine, John. I met up with some friends when you'd gone. We are on our way to get something to eat now. I'll catch up with you later."

Then the line went dead. Shadow winced as he replaced the receiver. Maggie's tone had been light and breezy, but he suspected that when a woman said she was absolutely fine, she meant the opposite. He had a feeling flowers might be in order. It looked like the chief constable wasn't the only female he needed to mend some fences with. Although somehow, he didn't think a bunch of freesias were going to do the trick with her. He stood up with a sigh. He may as well get it over with.

A few moments later and he was downstairs. He raised his hand and was about to knock, when the door to Superintendent Branston's old office opened and he found himself face to face with Sir Charles again.

"Ah, Shadow, there you are! Congratulations on a job well done," said the politician shaking him warmly by the hand. "I've just been singing your praises to the chief constable. The way you and your sergeant apprehended Siobhan with the minimum of disruption to the meeting was very impressive."

"Thank you very much, Sir Charles," replied Shadow glancing through the open doorway to the chief constable who was standing behind her desk wearing a tight smile that didn't reach her eyes.

"I always knew Siobhan was feisty, but I never had her down as a killer," continued Sir Charles, "but I understand her arrest also has implications for Sergeant Hedley and the case against him will no longer be pursued under the circumstances."

Shadow felt a wave of relief wash over him. "That's partly why this investigation has been so important to the team and perhaps why our methods have been a little unconventional," he explained for the benefit of the still-silent chief constable as much as the politician.

"Yes, it must have been difficult to have one of your own involved," sympathised Sir Charles. "The chief constable and I have been discussing the appointment of the new superintendent. I suggested promoting someone from within the station to avoid any more upset or upheaval. Clarkson would seem like the obvious choice. He is the most experienced of all the candidates after all."

"An excellent idea, Sir Charles," agreed Shadow. "Deputy Superintendent Clarkson is very well regarded by his fellow officers." The chief constable's smile was now so tight it was beginning to look like rigor mortis had set in.

"I wonder if you have a moment, Chief Inspector? There's another matter I'd like to discuss with you," asked the MP.

"Certainly, Sir Charles, unless the chief constable needs me?" replied Shadow.

His enquiry was met with nothing more than a sharp shake of the head from his boss, so he turned and followed Sir Charles down the corridor and out of the station into the car park. A Mercedes with blacked-out windows was parked in one of the visitor's spaces. Sir Charles opened the driver's door and motioned for Shadow to get in.

"I'll leave you two to have a chat," he said. Shadow slipped into the driver's seat and found he was sitting next to Annabel DeVere.

"Did Siobhan kill Flynn?" she asked without preamble.

Shadow shook his head. "No, she was at the racecourse all that afternoon."

"So, who did kill him?"

"We don't know yet." They sat in silence for a moment, until Shadow turned to her and asked, "Why didn't you tell us about you and Flynn?"

Annabel slowly shook her head as she continued to stare straight ahead. Her beautiful face was so pale, it looked like it had been carved out of alabaster.

"I don't know," she said quietly. "I think I was in shock. My whole world had just come crashing down. I was scared and I just wanted to get rid of you and for Bertie's damn party to be over, so I could be by myself. Charles said I should speak with you, but I couldn't face it. I switched to autopilot, pretending I was on a photo shoot, playing the part of a haughty hostess, when really I felt like a wounded animal that needed to crawl into a cave and lick her wounds. I'm sorry, I know I was rude."

Shadow nodded; one thing he did understand was the need to be alone. "Who else knew about your affair?"

"Flynn had told Siobhan about us a few days ago, but until then just Charles and Clancy. We'd been so careful, using untraceable phones and only meeting away from the village."

"Except when you met at Clancy's cottage."

"Yes, just over a week ago. It was a risk, but I'd found out I was pregnant that morning and had been trying to contact Flynn. He was at a race meeting all day, then I was meant to be attending another party, but I snuck out and met him at Clancy's. He was so happy when I told him." She smiled at the memory, then her smile faded. "If only we'd left Kirkdale that night, he'd still be here."

Shadow nodded. The saddest stories were full of 'if on-lys'. Although he felt like he was intruding upon Annabel's grief, now she was finally talking to him, he wanted to find out as much as possible.

"We found the mobile you used to call him on close to the murder scene," he said.

Annabel turned her face towards him and placed her hands protectively across her still flat stomach.

"I didn't call him that day. My phone was taken from me. I'd locked myself in my bathroom and turned the radio on, the day he died. My morning sickness was more like lunchtime sickness. I didn't want anyone to hear me. When I finally came out, someone had taken the phone from my bedroom. It was stupid of me. I was usually so careful. I always deleted any messages I sent or received on that phone and keep it hidden, but it needed charging and I thought everyone was out. Now I don't have any of his texts to me or even a recording of his voice."

A tear rolled silently down her cheek. Shadow rummaged through his pockets until he produced a slightly crumpled handkerchief. Annabel took it with a grateful smile and dabbed at her eyes.

"Whoever took your phone, used it to call Flynn."

Annabel stared at him in horror as she realised what he was saying. "You mean they used it to lure him to his death by pretending to be me?"

Shadow nodded.

"They called him on his main phone though, not the one he used to contact you."

"Nobody else knew the number for his other phone. I

knew it by heart, so I didn't keep a record of it anywhere."

"There is also the possibility somebody wanted to use your phone to implicate you. Do you have any enemies?"

Annabel gave a sharp laugh. "In Kirkdale? I think you'll struggle to find anyone who was happy about me marrying Bertie. They were all very content with the status quo. Having Bertie behave like the naughty little boy he always was, head of the estate in name only, while Sybil and Plum plotted and planned for the day Seb will inherit." Annabel sighed and rested her head against the back of the seat. "My husband isn't a bad person, Chief Inspector, but he's weak, easily led. He and I should never have married. We are too different but—" she paused "—I was tired of modelling. I'd been working since I was sixteen and I hated being constantly followed by the paparazzi, and yes, I admit I liked the idea of being a duchess and living in a castle. Sybil was still recovering, so for once Bertie didn't have her monitoring his every move. He liked the idea of being married to a famous model, but unfortunately not the reality. As soon as we arrived in Kirkdale he changed. It was as if he regressed to being a child again. The spoilt brat as Plum calls him."

"Did Flynn know about this scheme to switch the horses?"

"I don't know. Nobody ever mentioned it to me. He had handed over most of the day-to-day running of the stables to Siobhan. He had told her he wanted to leave and all she's ever cared about are her horses. She was going to buy him out. I wanted to get away as soon as possible and make a new start, but he was adamant that he wouldn't leave without selling the stables first. He said he wanted to be able to provide for our child. His own father had died when he was a baby, and he and his mother had often needed to rely on charity and the kindness of others. I understood that. We planned to leave after the last day of the York race meeting. He said Siobhan would have the money by then."

Shadow nodded. Now he finally had a motive for Siobhan switching the horses.

"We haven't ruled out the possibility Siobhan had an accomplice," he said. "Do you think your brother-in-law or husband could have shot Flynn, with the rest of the party covering for them?"

Annabel gave a firm shake of her head.

"No, Bertie can sometimes say cruel things, but he would never kill anyone. I wouldn't put it past Piers, but Charles was with them. There's no way he would have lied to me."

They both turned to look at the politician who was pacing up and down at the entrance of the car park with his hands in his pockets. He appeared to be deep in thought.

"He seems very fond of you," commented Shadow.

"He's been very kind. He saw how things were with Bertie and let Flynn and me meet in one of his cottages. I wouldn't have got through these last few days without him. I always joke that my knight wears a suit of navy pinstripe not shining armour," she said with a small smile. Shadow suddenly remembered something that had been bothering since he'd interviewed everyone at the castle.

"What did you and your sister talk about on the morning of the shoot?"

"Money. Lavinia needed to borrow some, quite a lot, more than I could get hold of. I told her I would have to speak to Bertie—I know he had bailed them out in the past—but later at the party, she told me to forget about it."

"I see, on the subject of money, did you sign a prenuptial agreement when you got married?"

Annabel shook her head.

"No, Chief Inspector, it was a bit of whirlwind wedding at Chelsea Registry Office with only Lavinia and Piers as witnesses. There wasn't time for anything like a prenup but—" she paused and looked him in the eye "—I would never take any money from Bertie. Like I said, if it had been up to me, Flynn and I would have left the village as soon as I found out I was pregnant."

"One more question. It's a little delicate, but I heard that your husband suffered from fertility problems."

Annabel rolled her eyes. "Oh, Sybil is convinced all Bertie's troubles go back to a bout of scarlet fever he had as a child. That's her excuse for still treating him like a little boy. Don't think I'm unsympathetic, Chief Inspector. I know it weakened his heart, but he refuses to follow advice; he's still smokes and drinks too much. As to whether if affected his fertility, I can't tell you, but the reason he and I didn't conceive isn't medical. Almost as soon as I moved into the castle, he barely came near me. I felt incredibly alone, then I met Flynn and as they say the rest is history."

CHAPTER TEN

Across 8. You can't hire the one to succeed you (4 letters)

S HADOW WATCHED SILENTLY as the Mercedes drove away. One part of the puzzle may had been solved but he still couldn't be sure who was responsible for FitzAllan's murder. There was a tap on his shoulder, and he turned to see Jimmy standing behind him.

"I thought I told you to go home."

"I was on my way, Chief, but Siobhan's solicitor has just turned up. Siobhan's been pretty rude to her. It doesn't sound like she's in the mood to cooperate. I thought you might want me to sit in on the interview with you—you know as I was the arresting officer." He pointed down to his feet. "I found some trainers in my locker. Oh, and the statement from the duke's solicitors has arrived," he said handing over a sheet of paper headed with the name and address of Dalrymple's firm. Shadow's eyes scanned the document picking out the relevant information from the legal jargon and elegant phrases, then sighed.

"It looks like Siobhan's on her own. Let's see if we can persuade her to speak."

THE TWO DETECTIVES entered the interview room. Siobhan was sitting behind the table with her arms folded and an expression on her face that could freeze water. The young woman next to her, wearing a dark grey suit, seemed a little flustered and was hurriedly flicking through the case notes in front on her. Shadow and Jimmy introduced themselves for the purpose of the recording before taking their seats.

"I have a statement from the Duke of Kirkdale's solicitor. It says he had no idea you planned to switch the identities of his two horses in the Heart of Yorkshire Cup and you acted without his authority."

Siobhan gave a snort louder than any of her horses. "Is that why Eastwold bet every penny he could lay his hands on?" she retorted before her solicitor could stop her.

"Are you saying they were involved? Did they ask you to alter the appearance of the horses?"

"What if they did? It's my word against theirs. Two against one. Now that Flynn and Aidan are dead, I'm on my own."

"So, you came up with this plan on your own. You risked the reputation of your stables because you needed the money so you could buy Flynn's share of the stables."

"And he could ride off into the sunset with Lady Penelope," snapped Siobhan, as her solicitor looked between the two of them and seemed to be struggling to follow the conversation.

"But when Flynn heard what you were planning, he wanted nothing to do with it, so you threatened Annabel instead. What were you going to do? Go to the press?"

"Flynn thought he was so clever with his secret little telephones, trying to protect that spoilt madam." Siobhan almost spat out the words.

"Why did you still go ahead with the plan when Flynn was killed? Surely the stables were all yours now."

Siobhan tossed her head back, her nostrils flaring and her eyes blazing with fury.

"I put my heart and soul into that place. Flynn might have his fancy qualifications, but nobody understands the horses like I do, nobody. But what did faithless, feckless Flynn do? Draw up a will leaving everything he owned to precious Annabel and his unborn child. The charlatan even told me what he'd done: 'When my father died he left me with nothing. I won't make the same mistake, Siobhan'," she repeated, putting on a simpering voice.

"And what about Aidan? With Flynn gone he would have nothing to do with the plan."

"I would like a moment alone with my client," said the solicitor quickly, but Siobhan ignored her.

"That jumped-up little traitor," she almost shrieked. "He'd have walked over hot coals to Dublin and back for Flynn, but when he heard he was dead he wouldn't so much as lift a finger to help me. Instead, he wanted a bribe to keep his mouth shut. Ungrateful sod."

"I understood the charge against my client was one of fraud," said the solicitor who was beginning to look worried.

"Fraud and the attempted murder of her employee Aidan O'Doyle," replied Jimmy helpfully, as the solicitor started rapidly flicking through her notes. Shadow continued to focus on Siobhan.

"It sounds like you think he deserved to die," he said. Siobhan's eyes were flashing angrily again. If he could push her enough, they might be able to get a confession.

"You don't need to answer that," said her solicitor swiftly.

"Were you angry with him because with Flynn gone, he wouldn't help you change the appearance of the two horses?"

"I didn't need his help," snorted Siobhan, "or Flynn's help. That's the problem with people: they all let you down in the end. You can't trust them, not like you can a horse."

The solicitor was growing paler by the second and looked very much as though she would like to gag her client.

"Parnell certainly didn't let you down when he carried you safely to York and back, so you could attack Aidan," said Shadow.

For a second, Siobhan's face softened at the mention of the animal.

"Who's Parnell?" asked the solicitor still clearly confused.

"Mrs FitzAllan's horse," supplied Jimmy.

"But not one of the horses involved in the accusation of

fraud?" queried the solicitor, while Siobhan's eyes were still fixed on Shadow.

"It was quite a risk travelling all that way on a horse, with no guarantee that you wouldn't be seen, and you very nearly weren't. We only managed to find one photo of him."

Shadow slid the picture Jimmy had found on social media across the table. Siobhan's eyes rested on it for a second, but her solicitor picked it up. "This doesn't prove my client was involved," she said.

Shadow ignored her and continued to address Siobhan. "Perhaps we've got it wrong. Maybe you are right and Kirkdale and Eastwold not only knew about the switch of horses, but it was their idea. Flynn and Aidan didn't want anything to do with it, so they had to be kept quiet."

"Flynn was nothing to do with me—you won't pin that on me. We washed our hands of each other long ago. As for Aidan, he deserved to have some sense knocked into that thick skull of his."

To his left Shadow heard his sergeant's sharp intake of breath and he allowed himself the briefest of smiles.

"We never released the details of how Mr O'Doyle was injured," he said calmly. As he'd hoped Siobhan's colourful use of language had given her away, just like when she'd first made him suspicious by saying Aidan was sprawled in the road. He turned to Jimmy. "As you were the arresting officer, I think you should do the honours."

He stood up and as he left the interview room, he felt a

sense of satisfaction as he heard Jimmy explain that they now believed they had enough evidence against Siobhan and would be sending the file to the Crown Prosecution Service, who would decide whether to charge her. Shadow knew he could leave his sergeant to deal with the paperwork alone and for once he was in the position to deliver some good news. He strode out of the police station and through the crowded streets. The air was still hot and muggy and the racegoers, now with ties loosened and high heels in hands rather than on feet, were thronging into the city's many bars and pubs, celebrating or commiserating.

Twenty minutes later he was knocking on George's front door. Carol ushered him through into the sitting room where George was still working through his old diaries. He stood up, his face a mixture of hope and apprehension. Shadow got straight to the point.

"We've arrested someone for the attempted murder of Aidan O'Doyle, and they have as good as confessed. The case against you is being dropped."

There was a muffled squeal behind him from Carol, whose hands had flown up to her face. George, however, slumped forward and buried his head in his hands. His shoulders began to silently shake. To Shadow's embarrassment he realised his old friend was sobbing.

"I'll go," he said quickly stepping back into the hallway.

Carol followed him to the doorway, but her eyes didn't leave her husband. "Do you have to rush off? I feel like we should celebrate," she whispered, her eyes glistening with tears.

Shadow gave her arm a squeeze. "There'll be time for that later when you've had chance to tell your daughters. He's been through hell; go and take care of him."

Carol gave him a quick hug. "Thank you, John," she said before hurrying back to George. Shadow let himself out and began the long walk back to *Florence*. He couldn't face spending another evening amongst the racing crowd, so he called into Sapori on Shambles for a takeaway pizza. As he carried it home, he thought about Annabel and how he'd been wrong about her. He had thought she was cold and aloof, but really she was alone and frightened. He considered how circumstances changed people. He remembered his mother as being serious and distant, but had she always been that way? If his father had lived, might she have been more fun and carefree? Would he have been a different person if he'd never lost Luisa?

BACK ON *FLORENCE* he sat outside eating his pizza and drinking wine as the voice of Frank Sinatra floated out from his ancient stereo. The geese gazed at him with their beady eyes from their position on the roof. He'd made the mistake of throwing them some of his pizza crust and now they were watching his every move.

He let his mind wander over the events of the last few days as it tried to make sense of everything. Very slowly things began to fall into place. The secret passages, Flynn's relationship with Annabel, the missing gun and his conversations with Seb, Clancy and Bet. The more he pondered the more certain he was that he now knew the identity of the killer. However, he was also sure he didn't have enough evidence to accuse let alone charge the person in question. There wasn't a chance the chief constable would let him bring his suspect in for questioning. He could picture her face if he even suggested it. No, he would have to come up with an idea she would find acceptable. Ironically, she had been right to keep the two incident rooms separate. Not that he could tell her that now.

He sat sipping his wine for another hour or so until he had come up with a plan he was happy with, then he stood up with a sense of satisfaction and looked over to his winged audience half expecting applause, but they were fast asleep.

"I FIND IT hard to believe you are seriously suggesting going to Kirkdale Castle after yesterday's escapade," exclaimed the chief constable at the other end of the phone line.

"Actually, ma'am, I thought I should go to the castle and update the family and their guests regarding our investigation. After all the inconvenience I've caused them, I thought it might be the polite thing to do."

His suggestion hung in the air for a moment, as she considered it before responding.

"Very well I suppose at least I'll know where you are today, but I don't want you going there alone. I shall inform His Grace and meet you there myself."

The silence at the end of the other end of the phone line told him their conversation was over. It wasn't quite the outcome he'd planned, but if the chief constable's presence was the price he had to pay for finding Flynn's killer, so be it.

FOR WHAT SHADOW hoped was the last time, Jimmy drove him through the countryside towards Kirkdale Castle. He briefly explained his plan to his sergeant on the way.

"Wow, Chief, if it works it really will be like one of those country house murder mysteries with the big reveal at the end."

"The key word there is if," grumbled Shadow, who was feeling unusually nervous. He only hoped Siobhan's arrest may have led to the killer dropping their guard. If not, he may as well retire now.

"Speaking of country houses," continued Jimmy cheerfully, "next weekend Sophie has booked a break at this huge stately home in the dales. It's been turned into a hotel and looks really nice: big open fires, four-poster beds and after-noon tea on the terrace. They even said we could take Fawkes, but Sophie said cats don't like to travel. Maggie said she'll call in and feed him for us. Isn't that kind of her?" Shadow merely grunted in response as Jimmy chattered on. "We're really supposed to be saving up for the wedding, but Sophie said we should use her winnings to treat ourselves. I'm really looking forward to it."

The two detectives drove on in silence for a few moments before Shadow finally spoke.

"I thought I should send Maggie some flowers. You know to apologise for leaving her so abruptly at the races."

Jimmy nodded but for once didn't say anything.

"Not enough?" queried Shadow. Jimmy shrugged awkwardly.

"I don't know, Chief. Sophie said she was pretty miffed that we disappeared like that with no explanation. She was helping us out after all."

Shadow thought for a moment before rummaging through his pockets for his phone, then he dialled three numbers. The first was the one was from the leaflet Sophie had given him for tickets to the Van Gogh exhibition, the second was for Catania where he ordered one of Gino's new picnic hampers and finally, he called La Scuola and asked Francesco if he and a guest could use his garden overlooking the Minster for a private lunch.

"Now I'll just have to hope she'll say yes," he sighed to

himself, then glanced across at Jimmy, who was now grinning broadly.

"Too much?"

"No, Chief, that's perfect. She'll be blown away."

"Hmm, perhaps." Shadow sighed. "I'll settle for appeased."

THEY PASSED TWO uniformed officers on the gate and found the chief constable was already there waiting when they arrived at the castle. They pulled up alongside her car and she led the way up to the front door. Jarvis answered the door and informed them politely but firmly that the family and their guests were due to have lunch in an hour. He then led them all towards the library and opened the double doors. Everyone was gathered there: Annabel, Sybil, Plum, Bertie, Seb and Sir Charles as well as Lord and Lady Eastwold. They all fell silent when they saw the three police officers. Shadow was relieved to see there was no sign of Jolyon, the London lawyer. The French doors were open as they had been the first time Shadow had visited the castle.

"Thank you all for gathering here together," the chief constable began, taking a seat next to Sir Charles.

"I didn't know we had a choice," grumbled Lord Eastwold, half a tumbler of whisky already in his hand.

"I thought you would like to be updated on the investigation into the death of Flynn FitzAllan," said Shadow.

"You've arrested and charged his wife, haven't you?" asked Lavinia.

"In connection to the Aidan O'Doyle case and also various charges of fraud and corruption," replied Shadow glancing at Lord Eastwold, who had suddenly turned rather pale. "However, she wasn't responsible for her husband's death."

"So, who was?" asked Sir Charles.

"Somebody who was concerned about the future of the estate."

Shadow had been pacing up and down, and now stopped in front of Seb. The young man looked up at him in surprise.

"You don't mean me?"

"You are the heir to the dukedom, aren't you?"

Out of the corner of his eye he could see the chief constable open her mouth, but Sir Charles placed a hand on her arm and whispered something.

"Yes, you know I am," stammered the young man.

"And you know how to use the Lumley gun. You showed me a picture of you holding it yourself."

"But why would I kill Flynn? I hardly knew him?"

"Chief Inspector, this is madness. Seb had nothing to do with Flynn's death," said Plum putting her hand on her son's shoulder. Shadow ignored her and continued addressing Seb.

"Are you seriously telling me that in such a close-knit

village, you hadn't heard the rumours that Flynn was having an affair with your aunt?"

"I say, Shadow!" exclaimed the duke, but Shadow's eyes remained fixed on Seb. The young man flushed bright red as he turned to look at Annabel, but she remained impassive.

"What's that go to do with me?"

"If Annabel left with Flynn, she'd be entitled to a hefty divorce settlement. She didn't sign a prenuptial agreement. Paying that so soon after paying the death duties for your grandfather and those due on your uncle's death, there wouldn't be much left for all your grand plans by the time the estate came to you. Much better to get rid of Flynn and try and frame Annabel. Kill two birds with one stone as it were. You told me you don't have an alibi for the time of the murder."

The chief constable looked as though she was about to speak again, but before she could, Sybil stood up.

"That's enough, Chief Inspector. I'll confess. Leave my grandson alone."

"Mummy! What are you saying?" exclaimed the duke. His mother ignored him and continued to address Shadow.

"I never thought you'd be so underhand, Chief Inspector. Not enough evidence against me?"

"Not enough to reach the charging threshold unfortunately," replied Shadow easily.

"But you knew I wouldn't let Seb suffer. How did you know it was me?"

"The gun."

"A mistake on my part. It never occurred to me that the man sent to investigate Flynn's death would be the son of poor PC Shadow. Please believe me when I tell you what happened that night was just a horrible accident."

"It's true, Shadow. It was an accident. A truly terrible accident."

Everyone turned to see who had spoken. Bill Greenwood stood on the terrace by the open French doors, his flat cap in his hands. He and Sybil exchanged a small smile.

"I know what you are probably thinking," continued the old gamekeeper, "that we shot him to shut him up, but we—"

"Not we, me," interrupted Sybil. "I panicked and fired without thinking. I'd only taken the damn gun with me as an excuse. Told the servants I was going out shooting rooks. After Bill had left me, I heard a shout, thought it was poachers and fired what was meant to be a warning shot."

"It wasn't the servants we should have worried about but my wife," said Bill. "She guessed what was going on and sent your father to find us. Thought people finding out would put a stop to it. She never saw any poachers."

"What happened to the gun?" asked Shadow coldly.

"I took it and the cartridges, wrapped them in plastic, then buried it in my veg patch," said Bill. "It's back there now."

The chief constable clicked her fingers at Jimmy.

"Sergeant, tell the two officers on guard at the gate to

start looking in the gatehouse vegetable patch for a gun," she ordered, and Jimmy obediently radioed to the officers at the end of the drive as Sybil continued to speak.

"I ran back here and made it look like there had been a burglary in the gunroom."

"What about Flynn? What did he ever do to you?" asked Annabel quietly. Sybil turned to look at her daughter-in-law with loathing.

"That man has been trouble since the day he was born," she replied coldly. "His father's death caused Xander to resign from the army, and he felt so guilty he kept going back to Ireland to see the son of the soldier who had been killed on his watch. He even brought scarlet fever back from there after one of his visits, and it nearly killed his own son. He paid for Flynn to become a vet, then set him up in business on our doorstep, always comparing him to poor Bertie."

"You were jealous," said Shadow simply. "Jealous of a young man, who was everything your own son wasn't— clever, charming, kind, adored by your husband—and you were jealous of Annabel taking your place here. You may have moved out for the sake of appearances, but you couldn't give up control of the estate. With the two of them out of the way you could return to—" he turned to Annabel "—how did you put it? The status quo."

Annabel nodded slowly. Sybil glared at her, before turning to Shadow.

"She has no idea of her responsibilities. The role of a duchess is to support the duke and produce an heir. She did neither. I'm not going to be here forever. What if she tried to pass off that child she's carrying as Bertie's? A FitzAllan inheriting Kirkdale!"

Annabel sprang to her feet and instinctively placed her hand over her stomach. Her face, so often inscrutable, was now full of anger as she spoke. "I had no intention of staying here and passing off my baby, as you put it. I couldn't wait to get away," she hissed. "If you hadn't interfered Flynn and I would have been gone by now. I'm not a coward like you. I would happily have thrown this all away for the man I loved, and I certainly didn't want any of Bertie's bloody money."

The two women stood glaring at each other, only inches apart. Annabel clenched and unclenched her fist. Shadow was about to step in, but Sir Charles stood up and placed a calming hand on Annabel's shoulder.

"Sit down, my dear, and think of the child," he said gently, then looked at Sybil and Bill. "I really think someone should advise the two of you to call a lawyer, before you say anything further," he said firmly.

Sybil, who had regained her usual calm, smiled politely. "Thank you for your concern, Sir Charles, but I'm quite happy to leave with the Chief Inspector. I only have one request. May I visit my greenhouse one last time?" Sybil asked, addressing Shadow.

"Of course, Your Grace," replied the chief constable

quickly, clearly flustered by the turn of events and determined to take back control.

"Sergeant Chang will accompany you," added Shadow.

"That won't be necessary," snapped the chief constable. Sybil nodded her thanks and slowly and steadily made her way through the French doors. She paused for a second and gently touched her faithful gamekeeper on the arm. The old man looked close to tears. He nodded at the rest of the room before turning to follow her.

A few moments passed in silence. Bertie and Seb both sat with their heads in their hands. Plum reached out to stroke her son's back. Sir Charles began pacing up and down. The chief constable attempted to make a comment about the weather to him, but he ignored her. Bertie glanced over to his wife.

"Is it true about you and Flynn?" he asked quietly. Annabel nodded. Shadow had felt quite sorry for him, as his wife and mother had talked about him as if he weren't there. Bertie took a sip of his drink.

"You might have waited until we'd had a child," he said. Shadow raised his eyes to the ceiling. All sympathy had disappeared. Annabel gave her husband a look of utter contempt.

"And how was that ever meant to happen when you haven't been near me in months? You're not exactly innocent yourself, Bertie!" she snapped.

The room was quiet for a few seconds before Bertie, his

face creased with concentration, spoke again. "I don't understand. Why was Mummy meeting old Greenwood in the woods all those years ago?"

"For heaven's sake, Bertie! Don't be so naïve. Why do you think?" hissed his sister.

"It's all very Lady Chatterley, isn't it?" Lavinia smirked and her husband snorted with laughter.

"Shut up, both of you," ordered Annabel.

Everyone fell silent again. The only sound in the room was the ticking of the ormolu clock on the mantelpiece. Shadow watched the ornamental gold hands as they moved slowly. Five minutes had passed. Annabel rose from perching on the edge of one of the sofas and strolled over to the library table. She poured herself a large glass of orange juice before turning to look at Shadow.

"I suppose you are aware that another of those stupid secret tunnels runs from the greenhouse to the gatehouses," she said casually.

"Annabel!" exclaimed her husband.

Annabel continued calmly. "The seventh duke had it installed so he could visit his mistress without anyone knowing. Which you have to admit is rather ironic."

"How can you be so disloyal to Mummy?" the duke demanded whilst still looking bewildered.

"That bitch! She killed the only man I loved and tried to frame me by stealing my phone. I don't owe her my loyalty and I'll be damned if I sit here and let her get away with murder."

The chief constable turned very pale.

Shadow had heard enough. "Don't just stand there, get after them," he bellowed to Jimmy. His sergeant returned after less than a minute.

"They've gone, Chief," he panted. Shadow resisted the urge to curse. At that moment, Jimmy's radio crackled, and he stepped outside again. A few seconds later he reappeared, and Shadow knew at once it was bad news.

"The two constables have found the gun, but while they were busy in the garden an elderly man and woman stole their patrol car," said Jimmy.

"For crying out loud!" exclaimed Shadow. "What were they thinking of leaving their keys in the ignition?" He turned to the others in the room. "Where might they have gone?"

"I'm sorry I can't think," added Plum with a shake of her head. "The estate is over fifty thousand acres. They could go anywhere."

Suddenly Shadow recalled his conversation with Sybil in the church graveyard and the photos Seb had shown him.

"Is she still able to fly a plane?" he asked. Plum nodded as her lip began to tremble.

"Yes. She's not meant to, but she's an excellent pilot."

"Mum, why are you helping them?" asked Seb, who was trying to choke back tears.

"Because I want them to find her and bring her back,"

replied Plum calmly then looking directly at Shadow: "I don't want her to do something stupid."

Shadow turned to Jimmy. "Put a call out to all vehicles in the area. I think they are heading to Sutton Bank," he ordered as he headed out of the door closely followed by Jimmy, talking quickly on the phone. They hurried out of the castle and to their car. Shadow had only just fastened his seat belt when Jimmy's foot hit the accelerator and the wheels spun on the gravel as they sped down the drive. They turned right through the village and Shadow could hear the wail of sirens as several marked cars headed in the same direction. He gripped the edge of his seat as Jimmy hurtled down the narrow twisting country lanes, his eyes fixed on the white horse carved into the chalk cliff, as it grew closer and closer.

When they reached the car park at Sutton Bank there were three police cars with their lights flashing and several officers standing around. Shadow stuck his head out of the window as it shrieked to a halt.

"What are you waiting for? Get up there," he demanded pointing to the steep steps that led to the top of the bank.

"Why do you think she's gone up there and not into the woodland?" asked Jimmy.

"Because there's a gliding club up there and she can fly a plane," snapped Shadow. "Keep going. The club is on top of the escarpment."

A few seconds later they arrived in the gliding club car

park where they found the stolen and now abandoned police car. Jimmy jumped out and started sprinting towards the other officers who had climbed to the top of the cliff. Shadow stepped out of the car and held up his hand to shield his eyes from the glare of the sun. Above him he could hear an ominous whirring sound. Suddenly Jimmy and the uniformed officers threw themselves to the ground as a small red plane flew over them and off the cliff. Shadow held his breath and watched as the little plane rose high in the sky, executed a perfect loop above the village before turning and swooping over their heads again and soaring into sky once more.

Then suddenly, with lightning speed, it came nosediving down to the gorse-covered moor. A second later there was a bang and a flash, then a plume of thick black smoke began to rise into the air. Jimmy and the others leapt to their feet and chased towards the site of the crash. They were stopped abruptly in their tracks by a second loud explosion. Shadow hurried over to where his fellow officers were shielding their faces from the blazing wreckage.

"Call the fire brigade and an ambulance, for what it's worth," he instructed Jimmy. "I'll call the chief constable. She can break the news to the family."

A LITTLE OVER an hour later, when the firefighters had

confirmed there were no survivors and the ambulance had taken away what remained of the charred bodies, Shadow and Jimmy drove back to the village at a much more sedate pace.

"What first made you think it was her?" asked Jimmy.

"That first day we met her outside the greenhouse and she didn't refer to Flynn by name, but called him 'the poor Irish gentleman'. That struck me as odd. She must have known him for years but didn't use his name. It was as though she wanted to distance herself from him. I also wondered why she was carrying a wax jacket on such a hot day and that huge trug of wildflowers. Bill told me she only used cultivated flowers for the displays she created for the party, so I think she had hidden the Lumley gun in the trug beneath the flowers after the shooting. The wax jacket was to protect her from the wetness of the tunnel and to camouflage her when she waited for Flynn in the copse."

Jimmy nodded. "And Bill was there when we first spoke to her too. Remember he picked up the trug? That's when he must have taken the gun back to his garden to hide it," he said.

"Probably," agreed Shadow. "Really it all came down to the gun. When we discovered the gun that killed Flynn's was the same one that killed my father, it made sense that someone who was around then had to be involved. We knew from those old photos that Sybil was a decent shot. She had the opportunity to take Annabel's telephone; she could easily have crept into the library from the garden, used the secret passageway to go upstairs unnoticed and gone into Annabel's bedroom while Annabel was unwell. Then there was Seb telling us he'd picked up his granny on the way back from taking photographs. That's when she must have been walking back to the village from the tunnel, having been sure to drop Annabel's phone where it could be easily found. Ironically, if Annabel hadn't been so careful to delete her messages, Sybil may have discovered that she and Flynn were planning on leaving and he may still be here." He paused for a moment as he considered what might have been. "I'm also fairly certain Sybil was the one who contacted the chief constable about her concerns regarding our presence. The police had backed off once during an investigation involving her family and she hoped it would happen again."

"And all because she was jealous of Flynn and Annabel."

"Jealous and bitter," agreed Shadow. "She had dedicated her life to the estate, but Bertie had never lived up to her expectations as an heir. She was growing old, and her health was failing, I think she was scared of no longer being able to control the estate and its future. Flynn had always been a thorn in her side, and she saw Annabel as a threat to her position. Her hatred made her irrational. I think she discovered the affair when Annabel met Flynn at Clancy's. She dropped a very heavy hint to me about Annabel finding something worth staying in the village for. Sybil thought Flynn and Annabel might put Seb's inheritance in jeopardy and so took the opportunity to try and remove them both by putting Flynn in his grave and Annabel in prison."

Jimmy sighed and shook his head.

"She hoped we'd think it was a crime of passion." He paused. "Hey, Chief, I was thinking while we were up at the castle… The way Sybil thought Annabel would pass off Flynn's child as Bertie's, do you think Plum or Bertie could really be Bill's child?"

Shadow held up his hands. "I don't know, and I don't want to know. I think we should definitely let those particular sleeping dogs lie."

They drove on in silence for a few minutes before Jimmy spoke again.

"Why do you think Sybil and Bill didn't run off together, like Flynn and Annabel planned to?" he asked.

Shadow shrugged. "Things were different back then and Bertie was only a baby, but I have a feeling my father's death was the real reason. They'd managed to hush up what happened, but the scandal around a duchess leaving her husband for a gamekeeper was bound to lead to awkward questions being asked, and the possibility of them both facing criminal charges."

"But they still loved each other, and Bill remained faithful to her after all these years. I guess they are together forever now," sighed Jimmy sounding wistful.

"Yes," replied Shadow quietly, "and Sybil got her final wish."

AS THEY APPROACHED Kirkdale, Shadow's phone began to ring. It was the custody desk.

"Pull over here," he ordered. "I don't want to risk losing the signal while I take this."

Jimmy obediently stopped opposite the pub and waited as Shadow answered the call and listened to what the custody sergeant had to say.

"Well, Chief?" asked Jimmy, as Shadow slipped his phone back into his pocket.

"It appears a night in the cells has given Siobhan a change of heart—either that or her solicitor has managed to make her see sense. In exchange for us lowering the charge from attempted murder to GBH, she is prepared to give evidence against Lord Eastwold. Apparently, switching the horses was all his idea, a way for him and Siobhan to make the money they both needed. He only told Bertie about it a few days before, made it sound like a huge joke."

"Not a very funny one for the other trainers and jockeys."

"No but as always, Bertie was happy to go along with his old friend. However, when Sybil got wind of the scheme, she didn't share his sense of humour. I expect she tried to put a stop to it, but Siobhan and Eastwold were determined to go ahead, hence the last-minute invite issued to their London lawyer."

"Bet was right about her always knowing what was going on. I guess when it comes to parenting there's a thin line between protecting and controlling, Chief," said Jimmy.

Shadow raised an eyebrow. "That's unusually astute of you, Sergeant. While you are in this philosophical mood why don't you go and arrest Eastwold. Those two constables on the gate can help if you need them. It might cheer them up after losing their car in front of the chief constable."

"Don't you want to come, Chief?"

"No, I'll get out here," said Shadow opening the car door. He'd spotted Sir Charles outside the pub, pacing up and down as he smoked a cigarette. "Come and collect me later."

He walked across the road and raised a hand in greeting to the politician.

"You can tell it's been a stressful day. I haven't had one of these in years," said Sir Charles taking another drag.

"You didn't feel like staying at the castle?"

"No, not when the news came through about Sybil and old Greenwood. It felt like I was intruding. The chief constable is taking Seb and Plum up to the crash site. I told Annabel I'd wait here for her while she packs her bags. She said she'd like to stay in the cottage where she used to meet Flynn for a while, until she decides what to do next. I imagine it holds happy memories for her. Where is your sergeant off too?" he asked as they watched Jimmy turn the car around and drive back towards the castle.

"He has an appointment with Lord Eastwold," explained Shadow.

Sir Charles gave a knowing smile. "I can't say I'm surprised. I didn't think for a minute Siobhan had acted alone."

"Poor Bertie." Shadow sighed. "It can't be easy for him. He's lost his wife, mother and best friend all in the same day."

"Don't feel too sorry for him, Shadow. I expect he'll find comfort where he does most nights." Sir Charles inclined his head towards the pub window, where the barmaid could be seen pulling pints.

"Bet?" asked Shadow incredulously. Sir Charles grinned.

"It's been going on for years. Where do you think Bertie was while we were all at La Scuola that night?"

As if sensing she was being watched, Bet looked up and gave them both a little wave.

"Oh, I know she's an outrageous flirt, and Sybil certainly didn't approve," continued Sir Charles as he stubbed out his cigarette, "but Bet's the only person who has never wanted Bertie to be any more than he is. Will you join me for a pint?"

"I'll be along in a minute," replied Shadow. He turned, walked a little way up the road, stepped through the gates into the churchyard and followed the narrow path that meandered between the graves. Stopping in front of the two simple headstones, he stooped down to remove the now wilting white roses from the graves of his parents and grandparents. He ran his fingers over his father's engraved name and brushed away a few specks of dust.

For a moment, he stood there silently with his head bowed. When he raised his eyes again, he saw a magpie perched on the headstone, his black and white head tilted to one side as he surveyed the chief inspector. With a small smile, Shadow saluted him, as his grandfather had taught him, then turned and headed back towards the sounds of life and laughter echoing out of the village pub.

THE END

Want more? Check out John Shadow's latest case in
A Roman Shadow!

Join Tule Publishing's newsletter for more great reads and weekly deals!

ACKNOWLEDGEMENTS

My thanks as always to the wonderful team at Tule: Jane Porter, Meghan Farrell, Cyndi Parent and Nikki Babri.

I was very lucky to work with three amazing editors again: Sinclair Sawhney, Helena Newton and Marlene Roberts. Many thanks for all your suggestions and your support.

A big thank you to Patrick Knowles for another beautiful book cover and to Lee Hyat for coordinating the design.

A Forgotten Shadow – Crossword

1.							2.		3.	
	/////	/////	/////	/////	/////	/////		/////		/////
	/////	/////	/////	/////	/////	/////		/////		/////
4.			/////	/////	/////	/////		/////		/////
			/////	/////	/////	/////		/////		/////
	/////	/////	5.							/////
	/////	/////								/////
	/////	/////	/////	/////	/////	/////		/////		/////
	/////	/////	/////	/////	/////	/////		/////		/////
	/////	/////	/////	/////	/////	/////	/////	/////		/////
/////	6.						7.	/////		/////
/////								/////		/////
/////		/////	/////	/////	/////	/////		/////		/////
/////		/////	/////	/////	/////	/////		/////		/////
/////		/////	/////	/////	/////	/////		/////		/////
/////		/////	/////	/////	/////	/////		/////		/////
/////		/////	/////	/////	/////	/////		/////		/////
/////		/////	/////	/////	/////	/////		/////		/////
8.			/////	/////	/////	/////	/////	/////		/////
			/////	/////	/////	/////	/////	/////		/////

Across

1. The upper class to the coast I carry (11 letters)
4. Initially Fred, Ian and Xander alter the odds in their favour (3 letters)
5. Ride the filly or stallion along the shore (5 letters)
6. Tim and Tom begin to put money on who they think will win (7 letters)
8. You can't hire the one to succeed you (4 letters)

Down

1. An infidelity when Fiona and Anthony are seen at the fair (6 letters)
2. Don't scare the horses or they won't win here (5 letters)
3. Yes Dr I count in the great outdoors (11 letters)
6. Beatrice uses Brie to get what she wants (5 letters)
7. Snug is the last thing you feel when they go bang! (4 letters)

A Forgotten Shadow – Crossword Solution

1. A	R	I	S	T	O	C	2. R	A	3. C	Y
F	/////	/////	/////	/////	/////	/////	A	/////	O	/////
4. F	I	X	/////	/////	/////	/////	C	/////	U	/////
A	/////	/////	5. H	O	R	S	E	/////	N	/////
I	/////	/////	/////	/////	/////	/////	S	/////	T	/////
R	/////	/////	/////	/////	/////	/////	/////	/////	R	/////
/////	6. B	E	T	T	I	N	7. G	/////	Y	/////
/////	R	/////	/////	/////	/////	/////	U	/////	S	/////
/////	I	/////	/////	/////	/////	/////	N	/////	I	/////
/////	B	/////	/////	/////	/////	/////	S	/////	D	/////
8. H	E	I	R	/////	/////	/////	/////	/////	E	/////

If you enjoyed *A Forgotten Shadow,*
you'll love the next book in…

THE CHIEF INSPECTOR SHADOW SERIES

Book 1: *A Long Shadow*

Book 2: *A Viking's Shadow*

Book 3: *A Ghostly Shadow*

Book 4: *A Roman Shadow*

Book 5: *A Forgotten Shadow*

Book 6: *A Christmas Shadow*
Coming in October 2022

Available now at your favorite online retailer!

ABOUT THE AUTHOR

H L Marsay always loved detective stories and promised herself that one day, she would write one too. She is lucky enough to live in York, a city full of history and mystery. When not writing, the five men in her life keep her busy – two sons, two dogs and one husband.

Thank you for reading

A FORGOTTEN SHADOW

If you enjoyed this book, you can find more from all our great authors at TulePublishing.com, or from your favorite online retailer.

TULE
PUBLISHING

Made in the USA
Middletown, DE
18 June 2024